In the Den of the Dragon

by Steve Stanton

SKYSONG SCIENCE FICTION
Published by Skysong Press
Established 1988

SKYSONG SCIENCE FICTION
Published by Skysong Press

Copyright © 1996 by Steve Stanton

All Rights Reserved. This book may not be reproduced in whole or in part, in print or electronic media, without permission from the Publisher. For information contact: Skysong Press, 35 Peter St. S., Orillia, ON L3V 5A8.

ISBN 0-9680502-0-4

Cover art copyright © 1996 by Steve Stanton.

"And there appeared a wonder in the heavens; and behold a great red dragon, having seven heads and ten horns, and seven crowns." Revelation 12:3

PART ONE

A sharp stab of pain. A cramp behind the knee. Harlin grimaced as the knots began to form in his legs, tiny little tremors like insects under his skin. He twisted in his restraining suit and drummed his fingers on the control keyboard at his side. Overtime again, and no one to blame but himself.

He'd almost had his rock cradled when a stray had come on the radar—almost home green with the goods. Navicomp had indicated a collision course, so he'd had to break. No sense risking his neck for one lousy space rock. Chalk another one up to the fractional probability, the impossible coincidence of random mechanics. The stray had just grazed his target, knocking it into a new corkscrew trajectory. Harlin had chased it anyway, had synched and snagged it with some fancy maneuvering and a good deal more luck than he was accustomed to—now he had to pay the price.

The biomeds and nurses considered it a psycho-physical irregularity, the official title was free-fall stress syndrome, the result of fatigue and the waning hypersensitivity drugs, but the asteroid miners on the belt knew it simply as space cramps and accepted it as another of many occupational hazards. Harlin had seen some bad cases down on the docks—convulsing spider miners with contorted faces, blood crusted on their lips. But he had nothing to worry about, he reminded himself again. He was only a couple hours over the limit, his rock was secure, his screen was green. Just a quick flight to Base and he could log in his shift. A good burn bath awaited him, and an ultrasonic massage to clear the Hyperstim out of his system, then a chance to relax in his bunk and watch the assay results on his overhead monitor. Good magnetics on this one. Some spots glittered like polished platinum when the sun hit them just right. Cobalt, chromium, titanium—any one of these treasures would make the difference.

If he could just stretch out a bit, maybe brush the sweaty brown curls off his forehead. If he could just scratch that infernal itch behind his left knee. Overtime again, with cramps on the way. Trapped in a bullet. A stripped-down, computerized tin can.

More like a coffin, Harlin mused.

They look like skulls, Marinda thought to herself. Rows and rows of pale craniums buried here deep underground, their severed necks gently washed with nutrient solution and growth hormones. An army of lettuce heads to fight the war against starvation, to keep the colonists alive and the mines at full production, to keep the smoke-eaters happy—the Transolar executives with their fat cigars.

She culled a bad head and dropped it in her recycle sack, marked it on her clipboard and continued her rounds. She moved gracefully with the low sliding step of her kind, never taking her magnetic soles more than a centimeter from the iron treadway. Her young hips swayed with blossoming femininity as she walked, an attribute she considered unforgivable for the daughter of a priest. Bad enough that her breasts had grown almost as large as an Earthwoman's, but to follow it up with a fat hourglass figure would be the ultimate indignity. You'd think such abnormalities would be bred out after four generations.

Tova crawled at a slow but relentless pace down the rocky crevice, deeper and deeper into the unregistered darkness below the copper-zinc mines and hydroponic farms, burrowing into the metal planetoid like a tiny worm under the skin of a ripe fruit. He wore thick gloves to protect his hands from the splintered rock, but his arms and legs were cut and bruised, his knees calloused and scarred. An electric lantern was clipped to his belt, but he did not use it—better to memorize his way in the dark. He would not have the luxury of a lantern with Security on his tail.

Harlin flipped on his com unit and winced as the Base chatter flooded his tiny crypt.

"Spider Seven to Strategic Metals Control," he signaled.

The reply was immediate: "Harlin, you vac-head, where in space are you? I've had you on Overdue since I got up this morning."

"Okay, Control, don't panic. I'm right here on your radar screen. I should be visual in a minute or two. That you, Eddi?"

"I was just getting ready to shoot you down for a stray, you cowboy. You know you're supposed to keep com open. I'll have to log a memo now. My guns are already mobilized. I told you last time."

"C'mon, Eddi. I'm way outside the sphere. You know the background noise drives me crazy. I can't concentrate with the com on. Give me a private beam and I'll keep you company all day."

"Don't make me quote regs, Spider Seven. Just don't cut it so close on your approach."

"Sorry," Harlin muttered wearily.

Eddi's voice came softer now, with a note of concern: "You sound a bit shaky. You sick?"

"Not bad. A bit tight. No memo this time?"

A sigh. "No memo, Harlin. You holding?"

"Yeah, just under max—good magnetics."

"That makes the cramps worthwhile, eh?"

"I hope so."

"Have you checked your chrono lately?"

"No."

"Does it help?"

"Not really."

Harlin's left leg began to tremble in its close-fitting plastifoam sheath. He tried pressing upward and bending the knee a fraction, which seemed to ease some discomfort. His other leg had gone completely numb.

"You're clear on the Main, Spider Seven. I have visual confirmation now. You're glistening like a palladium pendant. Some guys have all the luck." Eddi laughed, a nasal guffaw that sounded like static over the com. The sparkle could be ice, he knew, but Eddi had been on Control long enough to know how to treat a shaky miner on his way in. Besides, it could be platinum or its more valuable cousin rhodium. Everybody on the shift got a bonus when a lucky rock came in.

Marinda found her supervisor, Nell, peering worriedly over the collection of printouts on her desk, an expression almost of pain on her wraithlike face. Both women wore the standard disposable coveralls provided by Transolar, papery beige pajamas that hung loose and baggy on the thin supervisor and left ample room for even Marinda's fleshy curves.

"What have you got today, Mar? Any good news?" The elder woman held out a bony forearm.

"Lettuce and tomato melons," Marinda said as she handed in her clipboard. "Level Four, Ninety-one to Ninety-five. About twenty percent below optimum growth."

"The line?"

"Sluggish but still moving."

Nell shook her head and added Marinda's clipboard to the pile on her desk. "If we don't get more water soon the whole crop's going to wither and die." She stood up, a full head taller than the young girl, and slid a few steps to inspect a paper-cluttered bulletin board on the wall. She added a brief notation and scratched at her short bristly hair with the back of her pen.

"What about that father of yours, Mar? I hear he's pretty high up in the Guild. Can't they put some pressure on those smoke-eaters to get us a decent water supply down here?"

Marinda cleared her throat and fingered the heavy barrette that held her black-silk tresses in place. "I'm sure they're doing all they can to eliminate the crisis," she said.

The thin woman turned to face her. "Sometimes I wonder if they're doing anything at all. What can they know about real life in the deep tunnels? They sit up there on their double water rations and tell us to make sacrifices for the collective good. Sometimes I wonder."

"They keep the sacred ceremonies," Marinda offered in embarrassed defense. "Obeisance to Ra," she added.

"Myths and legends. Outdated traditions. You don't actually believe that religious stuff, do you? The virgin sacrifice?" The supervisor smiled. A joke perhaps.

Marinda stared at the floor, her face flushed. The virgin sacrifice? "I don't know," she murmured. Some things were kept secret even from the daughter of a priest.

"Hey, I was just kidding," Nell offered with a chuckle. "Of course we all belong to the Guild. You know that." She came around her desk and patted Marinda on the shoulder, turned her toward the door. "You tell your father he's doing a great job. Ten percent more water, that's all we need. Just to keep the line moving. Give the Dragon an extra virgin this year if it will help." She grinned as she ushered the young inspector from the room, sure that the Guild, curse their bureaucratic souls, would allow her this harmless diversion with the preacher's kid.

The pleasure was excruciating, electric, eternal—the icy fire of liquid light pulsing in his veins. Pure, sensuous, sybaritic waves coursed from his chest to tingle along his arms and legs, to dance into his fingers and toes, filling his soul with sweet songs of surrender. His meager consciousness held no room for anything else—only the moment of infinite ecstasy, the endless orgasm of body and spirit.

Chairman Exeter Englehart was wired for pleasure. A tiny filament ran from the computer implant in his frontal lobe down through the more primitive part of the cerebrum known as the limbic system to a special area in the lateral hypothalamus, the reward center of the brain. Because the inner targets were a miracle of both complexity and redundancy, the precise point of stimulation varied widely with each individual, and the fine adjustments had to be made by surgical trial and error, a painless though occasionally frightening procedure. But Exeter was more than happy with his personal electrode placement, and indeed spent a measurable proportion of his waking hours under the pleasure wire. As Chairman of the Ra Guild Central Committee, he had numerous pressures and problems with which to cope. He used the wire to relieve tension. He used the wire to relieve boredom. He used the wire. It felt so good.

Harlin Riley stood in the doorway to the lounge and concentrated for a moment on the press of the floor against his feet, the slight tension in his muscular legs. Eighty-five percent earth-g here on the outermost level of the huge spinning wheel. The comforts of home. He lifted up his right foot and felt the ground pull it back down. He planted both feet firmly. As sturdy as a rock. Immovable.

The community lounge swarmed with spacers—biomeds in white linen, comtechs in grey polyester, spider miners in sky-blue jumpsuits. Scattered naval personnel in characteristic black uniforms milled among the regular crowd, off-duty crew from a docked Space Navy freighter.

"Hey, Prophet!" a voice called out above the chattering drone.

Harlin winced at the name—a private irritation between him and fellow spider miner Jim Nichols.

"Hey, Prophet! Over here." Nichols waved a meaty arm in the air, his blond hair wild above his high Nordic forehead. Another colleague, Eric Apa, sat with him, along with two unfamiliar young men in sky blue. They must be fresh recruits, Harlin decided, and as he got closer noticed that they both sported bright green hair. He hoped it wasn't contagious.

Eric made the introductions, calling Harlin "an old pro." Eight years in space, thirty-six from the womb, now suddenly old.

Harlin shook the proffered hands, thumbs-up spacer shake.

"Was that Ken Lamoosoo?" he asked as he sat down.

"Lamosieu," the young man repeated with a vaguely French accent. He had brown eyes, brown skin, possibly some African blood, but the green hair tended to obscure racial characteristics.

"What's with the lemon-lime hair?" Harlin addressed the other recruit—white skin, grey eyes. "New fashion?"

"Sure, everyone on Luna has green hair these days," Fred Carter replied. "Buy you a draft?"

"Just a citrus, thanks." Harlin signaled his order to the bartender and tried to imagine seven-hundred thousand people with green hair. A search for cultural identity, he supposed. Response to anomie. It made sense in a way. Colonists on Luna could never have the same goals and aspirations as Earthmen, their lives too far removed from the wife-and-kids-in-the-suburbs routine of middle-class luxury. So if they weren't Earthmen, who were they? Moonmen? Lunatics?

"What brings you two out to the belt?" Harlin asked with a smile as Fred signed for his drink. "Fame and fortune?"

"Just fortune," replied Ken Lamosieu. "The money sounded good."

"Good money, all right," Eric broke in, "but wait'll you see the bill for that beer you're drinking."

The five miners laughed heartily, though the joke was well worn and cut too close to the heart. There was nothing more expensive than imported mass in the belt, and the trappings of civilization came with exorbitant price tags. Rumor had it that Eric was in fact under some pressure financially and in dire need of a lucky rock, though he had bankrolled a long list of relatives Earthside over the years. With short black hair and finely chiseled Italian jaw, he looked as though he had just stepped off a shaving commercial on the holo.

"Speaking of money," he continued, "I hear you plucked a nice rock last shift, Harlin."

"Prelim looks good." Harlin grinned. "An iron for sure. Trace counts for cobalt and manganese."

"Sure took your time coming in," big Jim Nichols observed in a sluggish drawl. Nichols had brought in a "dirtball" last shift—almost pure silica and utterly worthless—and had been drinking steadily all afternoon as a result. "Have some trouble?"

Harlin nodded grimly. "A stray clipped my rock just as I was set to cradle. Blew my synch completely."

"What?" Ken exclaimed. "You had a collision mid-maneuver and still brought your rock in? I don't believe it."

Harlin shrugged muscular shoulders. "I was out over a full cycle. I just started from scratch on the new trajectory."

"Great space! I didn't have that one on my simulation runs."

"Well, it looked like a decent chase. My credits were down. You know how the Company gets when production lags."

"No one would have blamed you if you let it go," Eric pointed out.

"Green truth," Ken stated flatly. "I'm coming in every half cycle, rock or not."

Harlin nodded. He'd heard that line before, straight out of the Station regs. He'd even said it himself once, long ago. He began to feel old. What was he doing out here anyway?

"Yeah, well." He shrugged. "It looked like a decent chase."

In some places the passageway grew so small that Tova could barely squeeze his thin frame through the opening. Sometimes he snagged himself briefly on the jagged rock and had to fight back panic as he struggled to free himself. A slow death waited for the man lodged headfirst in the tunnels, a short funeral by statistic—another colonist buried deep in the caverns of Ceres, trapped in a rocky crevice or suffocated in a poisonous sinkhole where heavy gases accumulated like cancerous growths, speared on a razor spire or simply lost in the craggy maze of uncharted tunnels. Danger waited patiently in this black hell like a stealthy predator lurking in the dark, ready to pounce on the warm-blooded strangers who dared to explore the abyss.

Tova knew the risks. He had considered and rejected the easy path through life, the lazy glide toward apathy, and had chosen instead to gamble with death in the company of his Fraternity brothers, to shape destiny rather than succumb to fate. Though many considered him fearless, in truth Tova knew fear intimately. Fear hovered around him like an ever-present shadow, a bony specter to mirror his own frail stature. The coward turns when fear closes in, but the courageous man while being afraid stays true to his purpose. Fear is no enemy to the valiant warrior; fear is the warning voice, the trusted advisor. Fear is the beginning of wisdom.

"So why are you called Prophet?" Fred Carter asked as he set his half-empty mug on the table.

Jim Nichols picked up his own mug and smiled into it. "Yeah, tell them about your sprite, Prophet," he prodded, then turned to the recruits with a patently innocent air. "Harlin's got one of those little alien ghosties in his brain," he told them. "Like a pet, you know. Only we don't know yet who's the pet and who the master." He laughed, the conquering Viking.

The recruits stared at Harlin wide-eyed. Eric Apa looked uncomfortably at his hands and rubbed a scab on his thumb.

"Red flash," Fred drawled, shaking his head.

"No, really," Jim maintained. "I carried one myself once, believe it or not. My mother had it planted when I was a kid. Course I had it removed as soon as I realized the truth. Not the Prophet though. He's going right to the wall with his. What do you think? You got room in your head for a baby parasite?"

"C'mon, lay off, Jim," Eric muttered.

"Green?" asked Fred.

"It's not like he says," Harlin replied.

"You callin' me a liar, Prophet?"

"So does it talk to you or something?" Ken asked. "What does it say?"

"It doesn't say anything. It's just there watching."

"Red flash, man," Jim interjected. "What about the Manual?"

"Well, yeah," Harlin admitted, "there's been some communication, but not to me personally."

"These sprites are gonna take over, I tell ya. They're sending out spies to plan their attack."

"Bloody red," Harlin countered. "The sprites don't need our universe. They live in a different dimension. Outside of space and time."

Fred whistled. "Heavy tech."

"I think I'd prefer a computer implant," Ken offered. "At least then you know what you're getting."

"Yeah," Eric jumped in defensively, "it's no worse than an implant. Jim just likes to ride him. We've been out in the belt too long. Space happy, you know." He lifted up a full beer stein. "Space happy?"

The miners raised their glasses.

"Space happy," they repeated, and tipped up four golden brews and one citrus punch.

"Politics," Morvick muttered to himself as he twisted his hands in his priestly robes. "Unholy ecclesiastic politics." Like living inside a glass cage, he was always open to view yet constrained on every side. Every movement carried with it a winding trail of ramifications, a tangled web of expectations. The long road to the upper echelon banked and twisted with trouble, the high price of power, of obedience to Ra. The Guild was testing his loyalty by choosing his daughter for the sacrifice—a crucial test, a crossroad gambit. His only daughter, the mirror image of her dead mother.

He stroked his grey whiskers with long slender fingers. He scratched convulsively at the wiry grey matt under his chin, lower lip over upper and head tilted skyward. His loose crimson sleeve fell down his arm to reveal bony wrist and forearm dusted with fine grey hair like cobwebs. He pulled a gold chain at his neck to retrieve the key slung deep in his robes. He slipped it in the antique lock to open his secret cloister and stepped into darkness to commune with the Dragon.

The life was in the blood, spurting red and luscious on the polished stone altar. Morvick had been a sacrificial attendant once, had seen the life drain quietly away in the ceremonial silence—a quick and painless death, the ultimate union with god. Ra came closer than a heartbeat during the crucial moment, indwelling both hostess and servants, the Dragon himself guiding the knives. Such a beautiful ordinance, one sacrifice to save so many—it had a simple perfection to it, a solemn dignity.

What higher calling, what better reason for which to give one's life—to be made perfect and make others perfect? Marinda was more than worthy of such blessing, Morvick admitted to himself. A healthy virgin without blemish, strong genetic stock from a reputable family, frankly beautiful and without deceit. She could realize no greater joy than to submit willingly to the sacrifice and witness firsthand the transcendent mystery of the ceremony. Blessed forever in eternal reaches, she would rule as a queen of the holy city in a resurrected body of pure perfect light.

But she was too headstrong to listen. Morvick sighed as he considered his plight. She was a rebel at heart, a pioneer with a questioning spirit. It was his own fault, he knew. He had wanted to give her confidence, to make her strong and ambitious like himself. He had been too successful; she was too much her own woman now. How could he have known the convoluted trail Ra would take him on?

Marinda had already shown signs of suspicion. The time had arrived to examine the facts and calculate the best course of action. The crown of success fit tightly to the brow, barbed with thorns—had he expected less? The executive hierarchy was within reach and all else was relative. Should he confront Marinda now and try to explain? Could she possibly understand without years of religious discipline? Or should he take her by surprise on the day of the ceremony, kicking and biting all the way to the sacrificial chamber? Morvick lit the candles in the inner sanctum of his secret quarters and quietly prayed to Ra for guidance. As the flames faltered and Morvick's brain began to suffer the effects of oxygen deprivation, he drifted into a visionary delirium.

No mortal troubles under the wire, no lingering doubts, no sense of time sliding effortlessly by—just the superhuman ecstasy, eternal like Ra himself. In divine imitation Exeter practised his sweet duty, thus sharing the sacred essence, sanctifying his frail spirit to the all-powerful Dragon—any excuse to get under the wire. For countless eons he rode the storm-tossed sea of sensation, rocking prayerfully back and forth with the waves of pleasure, moaning rhythmically like a lover in the grip of passion. In the outer office, his secretary Lamarr worked through a pile of paperwork, undisturbed by the sounds from the Chairman's office. A dutiful and devoted servant, Lamarr had learned the art of aural discretion long ago.

When the timer gave signal, the tiny implant in the Chairman's forehead switched off the trickle of current, for Exeter would never, could never have turned it off of his own accord. He would starve first, he would die in his own wastes, a grinning skeleton. Reluctantly the Chairman surfaced as from a deep sleep. He tried instinctively to call back the waves of delight, struggled to imitate them with his imagination, but the sensation had deserted him. He felt empty, incomplete, hungry for the wire.

He need only thought-command the proper code sequence to initiate another two-minute session—a quick fix, a personal heaven closer than his fingertips. The Chairman considered this as an emaciated man might consider a loaf of freshly baked bread lavished with garlic butter and cheddar cheese. He stared at the scattered documents on his desk, reports on the rebel Fraternity, financial updates, and pondered his official duties. He was the only native on Ceres with a computer implant, and had negotiated long and hard to obtain it. Most of the top men from Transolar had implants, but not many were wired for pleasure; it was considered too debilitating for a busy executive. Exeter Englehart knew where his priorities lay. He settled back in his chair and slipped under the wire.

"Have you ever stopped to examine his point of view, Harlin? You know, looked at yourself from the outside?"

Eric leaned back in his chair and propped his feet up on Harlin's narrow cot.

"He thinks with his head, not his heart," Harlin answered, reclining, staring at the blank monitor above him.

"Is that so bad? To reason with the mind?"

"Not everything is amenable to reason."

"Perhaps not, but you can't live your life in a dream, without foundation."

"A sprite is no dream, Eric."

"I didn't say that. I know they're real. But I've never understood what they are."

Harlin raised empty palms up. "Neither have I."

"That's just it. You're running on blind faith here. Doesn't it scare you sometimes?"

"I know what I'm doing. You've seen my scraps from the Manual."

"Four or five pages from a book that may not even exist? You call that assurance? You're willing to bet your life on that?"

"Well, what are you betting your life on?"

Eric sighed, shook his head. "Okay, you've got something. I'll admit that. And it's intriguing, I'll admit that too. But great space, Harlin, it could be dangerous. There's something living in your brain, for heaven's sake, and you don't even know what it is. Did you ever see the old storybook holo where the aliens' instruction manual turns out to be a cookbook?"

"Look, you and Jim can talk about it all you want. And make jokes in front of the femmes and the recruits in the lounge. But I'm going to find out the truth. It's important to me. More important than all the chromium in the belt, more important than all those Earthside grounders living in that chemical stew, more important even than my own life, if it comes to that. Just stay clear if it bothers you. That's why I came out here in the first place—to get away."

Eric held up his hands as if to ward off the words. "Okay, slow down. I'm your friend, right? Wasn't I on your side in the lounge? I admire your stand. Sometimes I wish I had the guts to do it myself."

"Why don't you then? What's holding you back?" Harlin swung his legs off his bunk and sat up. "If there's truth in the universe, don't you want to know about it? Be part of it? We're never going to get out of this solar system sub-light. We're never going to discover all the answers without the sprites to help us. They can go anywhere. I think they might already exist everywhere at once. Don't you see how puny we are without them? They can offer us everything, the galaxy, immortality. How can you pass it up?"

Eric rose to his feet. "That's your trouble, Harlin. You're too pushy. You think that just because you make a risky decision everyone else should follow your example. The sprites are using people like you to evangelize the human race. They're tampering with your mind." He held out a warning finger. "You almost had me convinced once, till Jim explained the sprites' methods. I'm not going to be part of some alien plan of conquest."

"Red flash, Eric."

"Maybe it's not true. Maybe what you say is green. But I'm not going to jump into a nightmare without a decent reason. Show me some proof, Harlin. Show me some good old-fashioned rational evidence."

"The sprites aren't going to do miracles for you like a dog performing tricks."

"Then they don't need me bad enough." Eric started toward the door.

"They don't need you at all, Eric. You need them."

"I'm doing fine on my own, thanks," he said as he stepped into the hallway.

Harlin hung his head and scratched at a tangle of brown curl behind his ear. Maybe he wasn't doing the right thing. Certainly he had nothing to show for his years as a sprite carrier. One by one he'd driven away family and friends. Step by step he'd retreated into space—first Luna, then on to Eros, finally to Base Station just inside Jupiter. He had no place left to run now, and not a friend left in the universe. Just a few pages of hand-copied looseleaf and an invisible hitchhiker in his head. And vague promise of something more.

In a cloud of uncertainty Marinda glided down the tunnel. How complicated faith really was once you scratched below the surface. If only she could reach out and untangle the obfuscating doctrines like a snarl of hydroponic lines. If only she could see everything clearly at a glance. Naturally all religions pile up extraneous doctrine over the ages, but what kernels of truth lie hidden underneath like shiny diamonds in black hills of coal? What is to be revered and what feared? Why did the priests look at her as though she was a rare fruit being inspected for blemish? Why did they whisper about her behind her back? Not one of them would look her straight in the eye.

She remembered her first trip to the surface of the asteroid, to the glassed-in observation deck at the top of her world. She'd curled her child's hand in her father's flowing scarlet robes—her father the giant, the sturdy tower. She'd stared out at the stars with child's eyes and seen only holes in the ceiling—tiny holes for children to crawl through—and had wondered what could possibly lie beyond. A gloriously bright place, she'd imagined, a place for Ra and the other gods.

Now she wished she had paid more attention to her religious lessons. She couldn't even recall the basic catechism now. She had always relied on her membership in the Guild and her father's position, convinced that the daughter of a priest could never come to any harm. But where was her guardian angel now? Why did the annual virgin sacrifice seem suddenly so ominous?

With taut muscles and trembling hands Marinda slipped quietly into her father's secret cloister, having picked the lock, having broken faith with her god. She sniffed stale air and squinted into the darkness as her eyes adjusted to the gloom. A statue crouched in a shrinelike depression in the rock, a crude copper dragon standing erect on squat haunches. Crimson jewels peered out of recessed sockets, and a sneering mouth revealed long canine teeth with tips filed to sharp points. Six arms each ended in three hooked talons, and four tall red candles stood round the icon like sentries at the four corners of the world. Revulsion twisted in Marinda's stomach as she examined the blackened candlewicks—the evil flame had squandered oxygen here, the deadly foe been harbored by her own dear father.

Was this the benevolent god who provided food and fertility to all? Was this the master of the heavens who guided the stars and planets on their courses? Protector of the innocent? Lover of children? Marinda gazed at the statue as though entranced. The eyes must glow when the candles are lit, she considered as she drifted into herself, beyond herself.

After a time she blinked and shook her head to banish the strange reverie. Deliberately she moved her attention elsewhere. On the opposite side of the room stood a desk and chair, a cluttered bookshelf above filled with crudely bound, handwritten journals. She investigated with great care, replacing everything she handled in its original position. Attendance records, sermon notes, routine church documents. She felt a prickling at the base of her neck and turned quickly to look over her shoulder. The dragon's red eyes stared back, and Marinda shuddered to think of her father drafting his lovely sermons about peace and harmony with this terrible statue influencing his thoughts.

She turned away again to resume her search and found at last a slim journal titled *The Virgin Sacrifice*. She took a deep breath and opened the flyleaf. She thumbed through handwritten pages in disbelief. A drop of sweat fell from the end of her nose and stained the list of names inside. She cursed and wiped her brow. As the drips became tears she closed the journal and put it back on the bookshelf.

Harlin stretched out his last spider leg and drilled in his anchor. His screen flashed green. Rock secure. A smaller rock, about ninety meters in diameter, but a good iron. A few strays drifted nearby on the radar, but none close enough to disrupt his maneuvers. Harlin smiled as he angled his boosters anti-spinward. Money in the bank. He had a long trip back to Base but would get in under time with any luck. If only he could stretch out these aching muscles.

He plotted his course as he killed rotation. It had been a good chase but he was way out of standard hunting ground. A lot of garbage in the area. A tricky route home. He punched it in and redirected his boosters. He flipped on the com.

Silence.

He checked the frequency and punched in signal amp.

Nothing.

A visceral clamp seemed to tighten in his abdomen. He turned slowly, dreamily, as though removed from his body and watching from a distance, to scan his long-range radar.

Nothing but strays and belt debris. Base Station was nowhere to be found.

He gasped for air as a wave of dizziness washed through him. He steadied his reeling mind. Think, he ordered himself. Could they possibly have blasted out of orbit without notice? Some emergency? Impossible. Too much mass. At best the crew could have evacuated in the lifeboats. At worst...

He keyed in a signal to open his porthole shutter. He stared out at eternal night and searched for any signs of life.

So cold out there. So quiet.

Eric, Eddi, Jim Nichols—all dead. Quick frozen like vac-pak dinners. All the pretty tech girls, the nurses, mechanics.

So cold out there. So quiet.

Harlin checked his air reserves and reset the mix for conservation. Two cycles at the most. He switched his radio to the emergency band and quickly dialed down the volume as the signal screeched.

"Eeeeeeeeeeyaawwk—from Pallas Central and can receive you with minimal time lag. Please signal if you are able. This is an automated survival search for any craft in the vicinity of Strategic Metals Base Station. We are broadcasting from Pallas Central and can receive you with minimal time lag. Please signal if you are able. Over."

During the pause Harlin thumbed his transmitter and twice repeated, "Spider Seven to Pallas Central."

The reply came a few seconds later, a woman's voice in place of the automated baritone: "This is Pallas Central. We are receiving a strong signal from you. Please repeat your call numbers."

"I'm not sure I have call numbers. They're probably in the computer somewhere. My name is Harlin Riley, if that's any help. Who's this?"

"My name is Armstrong, Florence, Mister Riley. It's a real pleasure to hear your voice."

"Call me Harlin, Armstrong Florence, and tell me what happened to my Base Station."

"I really can't say, Harlin. I've heard everything from a core meltdown to little green men. We may never know what caused the explosion. Can you tell us anything?"

"No, I seem to have missed the whole thing. I was working outside the perimeter..." Harlin lapsed into silence as it occurred to him that he could expect no miraculous rescue from this woman. Pallas was at least four or five days away at full thrust. He was going to die in this tin can after all.

"We've got a good fix on you now, Harlin. How many survivors do you have in your lifeboat?"

Harlin sighed. "I haven't got a lifeboat, Pallas Central. Just a spider with two days' air."

Silence stretched out around Harlin as Florence Armstrong spoke frantically with her supervisor on an inhouse line. The facts were inescapable: space was too big and atomic propulsion too slow. And Florence Armstrong suddenly found herself in the executioner's shoes. Press this button and the current will pass through the victim's body. Speak these words.

When she finally came back on the air a few minutes later, her meek and broken voice confirmed Harlin's worst suspicions.

"Harlin, this is Pallas Central again. We—uh— haven't been able to contact any other craft in your vicinity at the present time."

She's going to cry, Harlin thought to himself. She's going to break down.

"I understand," he said evenly. This was all going on tape, he reminded himself. This was his last contact with fellow humans, his last message to a civilization that had rejected him. He could think of nothing to say.

"I'm so sorry," Florence breathed into her microphone, feeling the ache of death in her throat, the emptiness of space eternal around her. A colleague's hand gripped her shoulder from behind to help support her burden, and she reached up to clutch his fingers spasmodically.

Harlin winced at the sound of her plaintive whisper, his own melancholy overshadowed by the acute embarrassment he felt for the poor woman. Torture enough for both of them, he decided, and switched off his com for the final time.

Cold and quiet he drifted, and a vast universe swallowed him like a dust mote, like a puff of sacrificial smoke in the wind, a brief scent of salt on the inland breeze.

"Just you and me now," Harlin said out loud. "Just you and me and the naked truth."

He knew from the Manual that the holy sprites never died, that they were not bound by timespace nor constrained by speed of light or antimatter reactions. He had memorized what scraps of the Manual he had chanced upon in his travels, handcopied doctrines passed by mnemonics and smuggled from place to place. He had heard the promise of eternal life.

What he did not know and could not fathom was what exactly survived the death of his body, what exactly the sprite carried with him from the corpse. A mind, a soul, memories, purpose? Would Harlin remain an individual, a conscious entity, or merely a vague recollection in the nethermost reaches of the sprite's consciousness? How closely was he intertwined with the eternal aspect of the symbiosis? Would death be the end or the beginning of Harlin Riley?

All the posturings and prayers had come to an end, the accouterment of life stripped away. Nothing left now but a naked, cold, hard kernel. A seed perhaps. Harlin closed his eyes and waited for the cramps to begin.

Andy McKay noticed his secretary, Valencia, bobbing and waving at the door to the conference room, her face red with apprehension. He finished the next paragraph of his presentation, pointed with a black-tipped pointer to the colorful charts on the easel beside him, and politely excused himself for a brief moment.

He stood a menacing six-foot-four, with a wild thatch of red hair sticking up higher still. He was Corporate Director of Interplanetary Systems Support of Luna City Free State, and was attempting to sell a billion-dollar waste and water reclamation project to a non-aligned group of eight finicky Chinese investors with extensive mining interests on the moon and elsewhere. He was not to be disturbed.

He smiled at his secretary as he ambled easily across the meeting room on his velcro slippers. She probably feared her job was on the line, if not their dinner date that evening, he considered. Poor girl, she was developing an ulcer.

"I'm terribly sorry, Mr. McKay," she whispered as he approached. "Mr. St. Ames said it was an emergency. Really, this time," she added, making it plain she had done her best to deter the caller. "He's on Intercom 3, ultra hush-hush."

"Very good, darling," Andy said when they were safely out of earshot. "I'll take it in my cubicle."

He ducked through his office door and folded himself into a swivel chair that was bolted to the floor. His computer screen was blank—a voice-only call. He picked up a black receiver.

"Ricky."

"Andy."

"What's up?"

"What's down, you mean. Strategic Metals is sinking like a shooting star. I'm recommending a complete bail out."

Andy arched his eyebrows in surprise. Rick St. Ames, his personal broker and chief investment advisor, was not given to rash moves in the market. They had been accumulating Strategic shares for many months in a favorable high-growth environment. They had not discussed any divestiture plans.

"My stock alone will kill the price," Andy said quietly, more to give himself time to think than to offer Rick any novel information. "Why the panic abort?"

"The less you know the better in this case, my friend."

Andy grimaced at the hint of trading scandal. Rick obviously knew something he wasn't supposed to know. That would mean court subpoenas and insider-trading tribunals and other irritating bureaucratic legalities. Andy's quick calculations put a value of just over a million dollars on his Strategic Metals stock in the nominal market range, probably less than twenty percent of that after a blowout.

"Sell," he said, and Rick pressed a button on the computer keypad in front of him. The first trade was logged in before Andy's receiver hit the cradle.

Perhaps religions weren't meant to be taken literally, Marinda considered. Perhaps the sacrifice was merely a symbolic ceremony, a dramatization. Wasn't it true that a person was judged according to the motives of his heart and not the exaggerated tales of yesteryear? Wouldn't an all-powerful god prefer life to death and happiness over misfortune? At Central Authority all secrets would be revealed. In the den of the Dragon she would discover the truth.

She stood like a defendant before the altar of injustice and stared down the expansive tunnel with its ornate red draperies and golden tassels. She moved easily down the treadway on her slim dancer's legs and stopped at the end. A giant double door towered a full five meters above her head—the shiny portals of a god. She fingered the stolen passkey in her pocket, her father's key, the final sacrilege. She checked the hallway again for guards. She began to perspire in her loose coveralls. Her heart pounded in her chest like a hammer on an iron anvil.

Her father had surely noticed the missing passkey by now, she thought. He was probably on his way already. Not much time.

She gasped as she entered the sacrificial chamber, a dimly lit grotto about thirty meters by ten. The Dragon himself stood at the far end of the cavern, a full seven meters high, the same rough copper cast as her father's tiny replica, the same monstrous pose, crimson eyes and grotesque, daggerlike teeth. Slowly she was drawn toward the statue as though bewitched. The Dragon seemed to beckon her closer: *Behold your God, little one, and tremble before me.*

Marinda panted hoarsely like an animal starved for air, her throat raspy and raw with anxiety. In front of the Dragon lay a polished stone slab with four knives placed carefully in the center, one pointing to each corner in the pattern of a cross, and for a flashing second Marinda saw herself on the altar, the knife descending, plunging into her throat. She blinked and the vision was gone, but the afterimage held her crippled, transfixed before the Dragon. Horror clawed at the back of her brain like sharp talons ripping through soft flesh.

"Did you do that?" she whispered, not daring yet to believe.

The statue's eyelids moved, closing like shutters and opening wide to reveal malefic red orbs the size of pumpkins, glowing with hate and the lust of centuries.

Marinda's spine went rigid like a cold steel shaft. She choked and gurgled in her throat, paralyzed by the eyes of Ra. The Dragon's fiery eyeballs rolled to the left, dragging Marinda's gaze toward a large cooking oven in the corner—complete with plates and utensils, meat cleavers and carving knives.

"No," she moaned. "It can't be true." She staggered back.

"We must have meat, dear," a voice said from behind—her father's voice, cool and calm. "Don't you see? The chosen ones must be kept strong to survive. It's the Dragon's way."

Marinda giggled at first, then began to laugh as hysteria took control. She accepted the madness gladly. Memories and mind cracked and crumbled, the pieces falling out and scattering on the floor like the discarded toys of a young child.

Chewing antacid tablets like popcorn, Rick St. Ames stared in disbelief at the flatscreen monitor in front of him. Fifty-six, fifty-five, fifty-four dollars a share. Strategic Metals was well out of its trading range and showing no sign of a floor. Andy was almost clean but was getting burned badly. There was little hope of an uptick, so everything was going at market. Other mining stocks were dropping in sympathy: Transolar off three and a quarter, International Titanium down two and seven-eights. Space Navy Corporation, the huge transportation conglomerate, dropped an unprecedented five dollars a share in the first two hours of trading. Volume began to escalate as automatic trading programs kicked in. Luna Exchange had never seen such carnage, as rumor mills churned in an information vacuum.

What a stroke of luck, Rick considered, getting that tip from Lydia Neil in the radio room at Strategic Metals.

She'd wanted to sell the shares in her Employee Stock Plan, fast, and Rick had wheedled the whole scenario out of her—Strategic Metals Base Station had disappeared with all hands lost. Vaporized, completely obliterated, who knew how or why?

"Love those ESP's," Rick whispered to himself. He ran nervous fingers through his thick green hair and began to plan his next move. He knew he could count on Lydia to keep quiet—her career would be history otherwise. Now he needed to drag out some old investment reports and doctor them to make Strategic look risky, then backdate them on the company computer to make it seem as though he had been following a logical investment strategy. He knew he could cover his tracks like always.

Forty-eight, forty-six, what a mess. Rick's trading program beeped completion as the last of Andy's shares went at forty-five and three-eights. Still Rick sat staring vacantly at his terminal, his fingers itchy for more action, his mind numb with the aftermath of anxiety. He whistled as the board came up no bid, asking thirty-three. As he watched, it dropped to thirty, still no bid. The Exchange finally filed a cease-trading order for "full public disclosure," but by then the newsfax was already humming to life with the news. The public was stunned. Stock holders were devastated. At just before the closing bell, Strategic Metals reopened at nineteen dollars a share, still falling.

Fifteen pairs of eyes glinted in the feeble light. The black rock glistened with condensation, some areas lightly frosted with ice, the hot and humid air from the gardens far above having gradually filtered down to cool here in the depths. A few puddles of stagnant water nestled among the tangled rock.

The men knew each other by sound and smell rather than by sight. They had been meeting regularly for two years in the deep caverns of Ceres, planning their quiet revolution. Rarely in the same place, never at the same hour, they conspired in a shifting netherworld of possibility.

"Ra has seized the girl and entranced her," spoke one voice, Leolin. "We should have enlisted her when we had the chance, and saved her such suffering."

"She is kept in her own home," Tova interrupted. "She is not suffering unduly."

"She is completely catatonic," Leolin continued. "I think she has been given a mindblock or powerful neural inhibitor. She could not acknowledge my presence and did not even blink when I pinched her arm. We certainly can't count on her cooperation in any rescue attempt."

Leolin was not his real name. The brothers didn't use their real names in the Fraternity, for each member led another life far above in the respectable world of conformity and submission, the world where Transolar and the Ra Guild ruled supreme.

"She is safe for now in the hands of the Guild," Tova announced. "No harm will come to her before the ceremony. Ra demands a perfect virgin without blemish and in good health. Whatever drugs are being administered will be discontinued at least thirty hours before the sacrifice. Now is not the time to interfere."

Tova's angular face was almost skeletal, his eyes mere slits, his nose hawkish. His voice reflected his revolutionary zeal, strong and commanding, a voice of one destined for authority. He was the leader, the guiding voice behind a number of Fraternity congregations in this quarter of the planetoid.

"We have yet no place to hide the girl anyway. We must make proper arrangements and wait for the appropriate time to act. Remember our priorities, brothers. What shall we gain by thwarting the Guild in this matter? We make ourselves a mere nuisance at best. And meanwhile Transolar robs us daily of our lifeblood. Countless tons of concentrate are blasted into space, and what do we get in return? We have not even water to bathe. Our children go hungry on strict bread rations. And how will it be when the last freighter lifts off with its last load of plundered treasure? You know as well as I, brothers. We shall be left behind like discarded slaves to scratch a living from the barren rock!"

"Amen, brother," a chorus of agreement echoed off the cavern walls.

"I say let's stop the onslaught now," Tova continued. "What have we accomplished so far? We block a mineshaft here, we disable a shuttle train there, but production continues unabated. I saw the tonnage figures just last cycle. Productivity is at an all-time high. Our planet is being systematically raped before our very eyes!"

Tova paused to let his words sink in as he surveyed the small group of black-suited rebels. They were good men, every last one competent in his field and trustworthy to the core. But how long before Transolar managed to infiltrate their coterie, before the traitor surfaced in their midst like a bad weed?

"The time has come, brothers. The time has come to go for the jugular, the central nexus of the monster machine. Let there be delay no longer; we've got to cripple the spaceport or die trying."

"Let's do it," a voice concurred from the shadows, and other men murmured their assent.

"What are you men saying?" asked Leolin. "Our fight is not with Transolar. It's the Ra Guild that hoards the wealth of Ceres instead of distributing it fairly to all. Without the spaceport we will all die in the darkness of our own ignorance."

"The two are intertwined like iron in the bedrock," suggested Tova. "It will take a fire to separate them."

"Politics is the answer," Leolin maintained, "not crude violence and wasted resources. Let us consider carefully before we agree to anything drastic."

All the men began talking at once, arguing quietly about their future course of action. Tova watched and listened, trying to gauge his support in this quarter, looking for any new and innovative ideas that might work into his master plan. He had no doubt that the spaceport would be the ultimate goal of the group. In his mind, every act to this point had been training for the true exercise of power—rerouting supplies, forging documents, influencing people in high places. These men had banded together because of one common interest, a fear of the future they all shared, and now like timely watered fruit they were ripening for harvest.

A pebble dropped in the distance.

The conversation stilled abruptly.

Itchy ears tasted the darkness.

A distant noise sounded again, an echo of something scraping on the rock.

"Security!" Out burst the hoarse whisper, warning of every man's private nightmare.

Glow lights switched off, and utter black swallowed the brothers as they scrambled for safety.

A laser flash exploded in the cavern, a brilliant beam of white light sputtering and crackling on the rock like a drop of water on boiling oil. Hot steam billowed through the chamber, scalding the men's faces as they ran for cover. A small patch of metallic ore glowed incandescent in the darkness that ensued.

Suddenly, from the opposite direction came another laser blast. A tortured human scream echoed off the rocks. The stench of burnt hair and flesh sickened the air.

With both main tunnels blocked, only two small crevices offered escape. One by one the men filed through cracks in the rock without a sound, without a trace of panic. In seconds they were well on their way to freedom through a network of uncharted passageways.

Tova, the leader, stayed behind to look after the wounded brother. He heard a raspy breath and headed quickly in that direction. He tried to keep low as he crawled along the wet rock, the razor edges ripping at his black coveralls, lacerating his skin underneath. Security would have infrared scanners for an operation like this, he knew. He could hear soldiers talking in the distance, moving steadily closer. By staying close to the two areas where the laser beams had heated the rock, Tova hoped to remain invisible even under infrared.

He wondered why Security hadn't bathed the area in bright light and laser blasts by now. They obviously thought the rebels were trapped and cowering, but why not ask for surrender and take them all prisoner? Perhaps they weren't taking prisoners, Tova considered, perhaps it was a simple extermination detail. He shivered and thought of his Fraternity brothers. All would be safely scattered by now, impossible to trace through the labyrinthine maze of rock—all but Tova and the wounded compatriot.

He found his brother moaning in the agony of charred flesh, choking and struggling with death. The stench was overpowering.

"Can you move?" he whispered.

"I'm dead," came the tortured reply, and with a sinking heart Tova recognized Leolin's voice.

"No, we've got plenty of time," Tova said as he reached out a hand and drew it back sticky with fluids.

"Do what is necessary," Leolin coughed.

"What shall I tell the men?" Tova asked as he squeezed out tears and drew his knife.

"I did not betray a brother," he whispered, "even unto death."

Tova's blade made its way to Leolin's neck and rested there.

"The spaceport," Leolin murmured, and was released quickly from life.

Tova's throat burned with acid as he made his escape in the inky black.

PART TWO

Commander Sylvia Chiminskaya stalked the bridge like a roaring lioness seeking whom she might devour. She wasn't regular Space Navy, but she had adopted for her crew the same black uniform with gold trim. She was immaculately dressed, her boots polished, her jacket buttoned up to the top with mandarin collar starched upright. She wore just a touch of makeup—the one vanity she allowed herself. Her dark brown hair was pulled tightly back in a bun behind her head, exposing her small ears and finely boned features. She was a study in perfection—not a hair out of place, not a wrinkle in all her clothing. She tried to run her ship in a similar manner. At the moment she was furious. She looked like a bird with something caught in its throat. Finally it came out.

"Dammit, Winton. How could we have missed it?"

Ray Winton looked up from his computer simulation, a young and gangly blond who'd made mincemeat out of all the technical exams at the Academy. As Chief Science

Officer on the Early Bird, he was currently sitting on the hot seat.

"There was no way we could have spotted it, Commander."

"Great space, mister. That's the reason we're out here. Just a few weeks off the construction dock with a billion dollars worth of hardware, and we miss our first big chance to prove ourselves useful. Space have mercy on us. Do you know how many fat butts I had to kiss to get this project off the ground?"

Winton smiled inwardly at the thought but kept a poker face and said nothing—no sense getting the Iron Lady even more riled than she already was. Everyone on board had wondered how in heaven she had secured funding of such magnitude, but no one had the guts to ask her pointblank. Somehow she had finagled money from several major multinationals and just about every political entity that had even a remote interest in space. She had research staff on board from a number of top-notch universities, and some of the finest apparatus in the solar system. She had a list of research contracts as long as her arm, dealing primarily with the asteroid belt but including such esoteric observations as the speed and direction of the tiny electrons and positive ions that make up the solar wind. The very existence of the Early Bird was a truly remarkable feat from a truly remarkable woman. It must be the Russian blood, Winton decided. She was not at all like the girls back home in Kansas.

"Have you logged that report yet, Winton?"

"Not quite completed, sir." The Chief Science Officer turned back to his computer terminal.

"Well, how long do you need for one simple report, mister? I don't need a whole history book."

Ray Winton swallowed hard as he felt the blood rushing to his face. He liked to take his time when he knew his report was going under a microscope—when he would be called to account for every imperfection. Curse the old girl anyway. No wonder she had never married. Who could possibly measure up to her perfect standards?

As if reading his thoughts, the Commander softened suddenly. "Look, Ray, you've gone over the data spinward and back. I've been watching simulations over your shoulder for an hour and its driving me crazy. Just give it to me straight without all the technical goop. What in space hit that mining station?"

Winton sighed. Time to put his stripes on the line. "I'm calling it a comet, sir, a fast-moving projectile from outside our solar system. A local retrograde stray seems too unlikely. A wild Jovian moon is my second guess, but spectral indicates high vapor content—water, methane, a lot of free hydrogen."

Commander Chiminskaya considered this for an instant before speaking. "If it was a comet, we should have seen it out past Saturn. The coma could have been spotted from back on Earth by a kid with binoculars."

"Yeah, the big comets are often charted well outside our solar system," Winton agreed, "but we use the same technical term for the small blocks of ice that occasionally wander by. The giant head and tail are caused by the heat of the sun and solar wind, but I think this particular comet may have entered our system in Jupiter's shadow, never allowing the gases a chance to evaporate. A small comet is invisible when it's still frozen."

"So they didn't even know what hit them?"

"Stations like that are sitting ducks by design. They're equipped with large guns to vaporize stray

41

asteroids before they can cause any damage. Their long range scanners are state-of-the-art. The absence of lifeboats in this case indicates that they only had a matter of seconds before impact. There was a Space Navy freighter on the dock that also didn't get away. The comet may have picked up some speed on a slingshot around Jupiter. It could have been moving at well over a million miles an hour. Even if it was only a few hundred meters in diameter, at that speed it wouldn't leave much debris. The antimatter reactor would have imploded upon impact and sucked a massive explosion into netherspace. Every human would have been killed instantly."

"Pallas Central has a fix on the only known survivor," the Commander said wistfully.

"I thought all hands were lost," Winton replied with a puzzled frown.

"No one's holding much hope for this fellow either. He's in one of those small mining craft—spiders, they're called."

Winton nodded. "Not much more air than a spacesuit."

The Commander grimaced, her teeth lightly clenched, and seemed lost in thought for a few moments. She'd freefloated in space herself more times than she cared to remember. She'd almost run out of air once, just a few thousand klicks from the moon, before a fiery-haired shuttle pilot picked her up in his half-derelict tug. They'd talked of God all the way back to Luna City.

"Don't count us out yet, Winton. I've already changed our deceleration curve." She turned to gauge his reaction.

"Red-line boost?" he asked stonily, betraying no alarm.

"Navicomp indicates we can arrive in plenty of time. The hard part is going to be slowing down enough to do anything when we get there."

"How long in the couches?"

"Seven hours approximate."

The Chief Science Officer shook his head. "The crew's not going to like that."

Commander Chiminskaya smiled. "I know," she said.

"Night Sky, we love to fly."

A fresh-faced young girl smiled enthusiastically at Rick St. Ames from behind her ticket podium. She was wearing a burgundy blazer with a big white ruffle bulging out below her neck. Her breast pocket sported the company emblem, an embroidered caricature of a space shuttle with the words NIGHT SKY INC. underneath.

"Rick St. Ames," he said. "I believe Andy McKay made an appointment for a business meeting.

The girl's level of animation rose another notch. "Oh, yes, Mr. St. Ames," she replied. "Our manager, Miss Diane, will be escorting you personally. If you'll just take a seat over there, I'll let her know you're here."

Rick followed her pointing finger and sat down in a black plastiglass chair to watch the girl in action. She spoke amiably with the next clients, an older couple dressed up for a dinner date. The plastiglass smile, Rick thought as he watched her face; she must paste it on in the morning and keep it in a jar beside her bunk at night.

Out of the corner of his eye he noticed Diane approaching from her office. She had traded her company jacket for a shiny black tuxedo pantsuit with a white ruffled front and black bow tie. He stood to greet her and when she extended her hand he raised it to his lips for a quick kiss.

"I had no idea we were going formal," he said with a mischievous grin.

"Andy requested our royal treatment package," she answered, still businesslike. "You must have made him some money this week," she added as she began leading him toward the shuttle docks.

"Not exactly," Rick said.

"Everyone else got slaughtered yesterday, from what I've heard. My retirement plans have been set back two years."

"You were holding Strategic?" Rick asked.

"Wasn't everybody?"

"You should have told me."

"I can't afford you, Rick."

"What are you thinking about retirement for anyway? You're barely twenty-nine."

Diane looked artfully askance at the handsome stockbroker. "You've been saying that for years. Don't you ever give up?"

Rick laughed. "How are you and Andy getting along? Has he popped the big question yet?"

"I think he's been under some financial pressure. His eyes have been wandering again."

"Oh."

"I think his new secretary is the latest."

"She's a bit young for him, don't you think?"

Diane remained silent, somewhat sullen.

"He loves you, Diane. These other girls are just adventures."

"Have I ever told you that you're a chauvinist pig, Rick?" she asked, staring at him with deadpan eyes.

"Wow, this royal treatment stuff is really something else. Does it cost extra?" Rick asked, his face alight with boyish charm.

Finally, Diane broke down and smiled. "Okay, you win," she said. "And don't you dare tell Andy I gave you a hard time. He's got enough problems."

"I couldn't cross you, honey. You know all my secrets." Rick laughed happily. He was feeling lightheaded after taking two purple anti-depressant pills at the closing bell—stressbusters, he called them.

Diane grabbed his elbow and veered him sharply to the left.

"This is our gate," she explained as she tapped a quick code on the door's keypad.

Six panels opened like an iris with a hiss of pneumatic pressure.

Inside sat Andy McKay with two lovely young ladies in matching tuxedo pantsuits. One had standard Luna-green hair and the other natural blonde. Andy in contrast, was dressed casually in black jump pants and a baggy grey sweatshirt. A caption on the front of his shirt read, I've Been Rich and I've Been Poor — Rich is Better!

Andy was a self-made millionaire. He'd started out hauling construction materials out of the Earth's deep gravity well with a second-hand Transolar castoff. He'd flown it himself, skipped meals, cheated on emergency equipment and backup supplies; he'd scrambled from contract to contract and tried to play with the big boys before his time. Now he owned a diversified empire of companies, including Night Sky Incorporated, a small but elegant limousine service on the moon.

"Rick, c'mon in." He waved him forward, then turned to the girls beside him. "This is our exalted guest, ladies." They both jumped up on cue and each grabbed one of Rick's elbows as he stepped inside.

Diane looked at Andy and rolled her eyes heavenward. Andy smiled and shrugged.

"Please buckle Mr. St. Ames in, girls," Diane instructed. "We'll be lifting off in thirty seconds." She grabbed a mike from the communications console on the wall and signaled the shuttle pilot.

Liftoff was barely a bump in the night at low lunar gravity, which made Night Sky a relatively inexpensive transport service to operate. Andy sometimes joked that all he needed was a pair of monkeys spraying aerosol cans out the back to launch from the moon. And with Luna City spreading out tentacles like an octopus, there was an increasing need of quick transport back and forth from the suburbs and satellites, in addition to the regular milk runs out to the mining colonies and factories that dotted the dusty lunar surface. But more than just a glorified taxi company, Night Sky offered a touch of class, a hint of romance, and provided an ideal location for private business meetings away from prying eyes and electronic eavesdropping.

Diane was Operations Manager and held a ten percent "incentive" ownership. She rarely worked night flights herself, unless personally requested by Andy, her long-time partner and friend. She'd followed on the coattails of his success, supporting him when the weather grew dark and ominous, consoling him when heavy clouds threw lightning at their fragile dreams, and celebrating when the silver linings spilled out in their laps.

After they were safely in orbit and lounging weightlessly on their couches, Diane got up to serve champagne in individual squeeze cartons to all five passengers.

Rick thanked her effusively, then turned to Andy. "Want to get business out of the way before I show the girls around?"

Andy spread big red hands. "We've got to justify the tax deduction somehow. I wonder whether we've got a buying opportunity in the market just now."

"Well, we've had quite a run-up these last few cycles. I'm not sure the psychology's right for complete exposure, especially in the small caps. I think we're in for a period of adjustment and consolidation, so I'm sticking with quality for the short term. I'm recommending Transolar."

"Transolar. No way." Andy shook his head.

"It's as safe as mothers' milk," Rick explained. "It dropped ten points in the crash without a single change in fundamentals."

"I've heard wild rumors about trouble on Ceres."

"Rumors come and go, Andy. Ceres is a stable breadwinner for Transolar. Profits are good and still rising. I know for a fact that a dividend increase is in the works."

"What do you know about the miners that live there?"

"The stick people?" Rick shrugged. "No more than you, I guess. They've been bio-engineered for the environment. They live underground with just a trace of gravity. They grow some of their own food but rely on imports for most staples—the same as us on Luna."

"We have rights on Luna."

"Rights?"

"We can vote and own property."

"I'm sure Transolar looks after the colonists properly. It's a first-class operation."

"The whole setup smacks of slavery."

Rick bristled at the suggestion. "Transolar spends a bundle every year sealing and pressurizing more cavern space. The whole asteroid is porous like a sponge. Do you know what it costs just to maintain life out there?"

"You said they were making a profit."

"Of course they make a profit. You make a profit before you get out of bed in the morning."

"Right."

Rick rubbed his forehead and glanced over at the two young lovelies waiting patiently for his attention. They looked a little worried at the turn of emotion in the cabin. Rick squeezed a shot of champagne between his lips. He turned back to Andy with his best plastiglass smile.

"Okay, Transolar is not right for you. I can live with that. It's your money. How about some old-fashioned frontier capitalism? If you want to take a flyer, I'm underwriting a new company in computer miniaturization next week. They've got a new process for zero-gravity manufacturing that they hope will reduce the size of a brain implant by fifty percent. I could fax your secretary the prospectus."

"Sure."

"Great." Rick took another sip of champagne.

"I need to get away, Rick. I've got a few things on my mind. Can you break for a couple of days for a trip Earthside? Have you ever been to Canada? Have you ever walked an untrammeled forest floor?"

Rick shook his head. "I can't get away. I've got to oversee this underwriting personally. Why not take Diane?" he asked.

At the sound of her name, Diane looked up from the vac-pak dinners she was arranging in a service alcove.

Andy waved the idea away with the back of his hand. "She's too civilized for that sort of thing," he explained.

"A couple mosquito bites and she'd be baying at the moon."

Diane poked her head around the corner. "Mosquito bites, what's that?"

Rick grinned. "Never mind," he told her. "You two should really get together on something, though, Andy. Maybe even a permanent arrangement."

Diane stared at Rick in awe. Andy looked momentarily confused. Even Rick felt strange as the words crossed his lips.

"Well," he said as he quickly pushed up and floated to the ceiling. "I think I'll take our young friends up to the room with a view." He winked at Andy. "We must be getting near the lights of General Metals."

From dream to dream he fought his way out of the oblivion of oxygen starvation. From days of youth below a netless hoop on the tenement basketball court, from the empty refrigerator of his college dormitory and his grey-walled study room, to his father's early funeral and the first fear he had felt upon meeting his own mortality face to face, the certainty of death. The old and dying religions of Earth had offered him social programs and community action to fill a bottomless void within, a spiritual vacuum, and he had turned away with a heart longing for more. He relived his first excitement upon discovering the alien sprites, eternal reaches suddenly within his grasp, vast possibilities, a universe unexplored. He relived his last few hours in the tight belly of a spider. Having surrendered to death and tasted the dark night of the soul, he returned now dream by dream, step by step, to life reborn.

He had always imagined death to be a serene experience, like sleeping in a softly falling Christmas snow, like riding a rainbow over clouds of glory to a great golden door set with jewels. He had never expected such a ghastly battle with the black shadow. His body's absolute unwillingness to die had astounded him. Two cycles alone with the cramps, muscles clenched like titanium struts, lungs aching with every empty breath, the reaper always another anguished prayer away. A man is reduced, humiliated by torture. Two cycles alone with the cramps. An ignominious end.

He woke with lingering panic, opened his eyes and spied an unfamiliar metal bulkhead, shivered with disbelief. He thought he was dead, perhaps destined for hell. He was floating freely and couldn't feel a thing, not a trace of gravity. He twisted his head, he turned, he reached. Finally he screamed.

Biomed attendants found him in hysterics, windmilling in his stasis chamber. Most had never seen a spacer so obviously dependent on gravity, and wondered privately whether he was an anachronism in an enlightened age or a sign of things to come. The official report read psychophysical trauma—it was a miracle the man was still alive, let alone functioning at peak efficiency. Two doctors and one graduate student were already planning to publish his case.

Harlin quieted down once the medical crew transferred him to a centrifugal section at one-quarter-g. He settled into his basket hammock while attendants began a battery of tests. He felt cheated and somehow tricked, the butt of a bad joke. He had prepared for death and been denied, had groveled in prayer for an end to his sufferings only to find a new beginning thrust upon him.

Mental configurations were still vastly out of synch. He knew he could never be the same again.

He made a pact with life once more, for better or for worse. He was, as near as he could tell, undamaged. He checked for his sprite and found the peaceful presence within, the quiet strength that carried him when all else failed, and in a few minutes he had reorganized his personality: Harlin Riley, survivor, ex-spider miner, refugee from the world.

"Where am I?" he asked the fluttering hands around him.

"Early Bird Space Observatory," came the masculine reply.

"You picked up my signal?"

"We've been in the couches all day," said a female voice.

"Right now you're the most expensive piece of cargo in the history of space travel," said the first voice. "How do you feel?"

"Terrible. I ache all over."

"We'll give you a muscle relaxant as soon as we check for cerebral damage. Do you notice any problems? Any ringing in your ears?"

"I think I'm okay."

"Do you remember the accident?"

"I was out chasing a rock. I didn't see a thing."

"And after that?"

"After that I waited."

The doctor coughed, a purely self-conscious mannerism—the air and his lungs were both crystal clear.

"You prefer gravity to weightlessness," he continued.

"Don't you?" Harlin replied.

"I've never worked null-g for an extended period."

"On Eros we had zero spin," Harlin told him. "Freefall both onshift and off. If you forget to strap in for sleep you can hurt yourself badly; you wake up in strange places. If you can't touch something you can't move. You fall forever."

The doctor nodded without comment and Harlin looked him in the eye for the first time.

"At least with gravity you've got something, you're not alone."

The doctor nodded again as though perhaps he understood Harlin's dark dreams, the nightmare tunnels down into his psyche.

"We're about twenty-five percent here," he said. "It's the best we can do."

"Still no anomalies on the scan," reported a female doctor. "No gross damage at all. I guess we're green."

A third technician in the distance added somewhat reluctant assent.

"All right, Mr. Riley," said the female doctor. "We'll sedate now and let your body's natural recuperative powers take over from here. Any more questions first?"

"No other survivors?" asked Harlin.

"None, I'm afraid. I'm sorry."

"And what happens now?"

"Strategic Metals will arrange your first-class return to Luna. Or Earth, if you prefer."

"You're not headed that way yourself."

"No, we're outward bound, fresh off the dock, Commander Chiminskaya at the helm."

"The Iron Lady," said Harlin.

"You've heard of her."

"Who hasn't?"

"She's been around the block, I guess."

52

Around the block, across the solar system, in and out of trouble, and preceded everywhere by tales of her exploits. A product of the Soviet Space Program, Sylvia Chiminskaya had spent her requisite five years in distinguished if uneventful service before signing on with Space Navy, where her public career began with a bang—a nuclear meltdown, in fact, homeward from Mars. She'd sent a white-hot engine room into the sun and, using only chemical stabilizers for maneuvering, had swung her crippled freighter into Earth orbit with half the crew in a makeshift brig. How to turn a charging rhino with a blowdryer, by Sylvia Chiminskaya. The newsfax reporters had played it to the hilt, particularly since it was the first case of attempted mutiny on record. Space Navy Control had awarded a Platinum Cross and a bonus of a full year's pay.

Had she retired from active service then, her reputation might have faded with the rest of history, the Iron Lady nickname been quickly forgotten, but less than two years later she hit the limelight again. Heavy-explosive mining on one of the smaller asteroids had altered the orbit enough to put it on a collision course with a sister rock, both asteroids, Genmet 5 and 7, with rich ore bodies and fully established mining colonies in place. Space Navy had been hired for emergency evacuation of all personnel. Commander Chiminskaya was first on the scene. Without official sanction and breaking every known rule of safe operation, the Iron Lady fitted her atomic freighter nose-first into an enlarged mine shaft and ordered full power on the boosters. The Chief Engineer quit on the spot, so she handled the computers herself and took personal responsibility for the entire incident. Though all but skeleton staff were asked to leave the ship, the entire crew chose to remain on board—an amazing vote of confidence. Fortunately the margins of error allowed a successful operation, and the asteroid was safely shunted out of the collision zone. The Chief Engineer was reinstated immediately, General Metals Incorporated demanded another Platinum Cross for the Commander, and Space Navy Control had little choice but to comply, though without a pay bonus this time. Some people held that the concept of spider mining had originated with this daring maneuver, but of course such an assertion was impossible to prove. Certainly no spider miner would dream of moving an asteroid the size of Genmet 5. In comparison to an interplanetary freighter, spiders were lilliputian.

Harlin couldn't help but be impressed by such a reputation, by a name that carried with it such unquestionable authority—and now to be rescued from death by a legend, to perhaps meet her face to face. The last he'd heard, she'd been retired to a desk, a Space Navy executive. Apparently she couldn't get the vacuum out of her blood.

Rick tore his eyes from his flatscreen monitor for an instant to grab a telephone receiver.

"Rick St. Ames," he barked.

"Hi, Rick. It's Diane."

"Ahh, your voice turns my heart to wax. What's up?"

"If you have a minute, I'd like to hire you."

"Just a sec." Rick finished tapping out a transit code and sent a report into the network. He cleared his monitor. "Okay."

"I'd like to sell my interest in Night Sky."

Rick winced. "I don't like the sound of this, Diane."

"I'm not doing it behind his back. I told him right up front."

"What'd he say to that?"

"He's very confused."

"So am I. Do you need some extra money for some reason?"

"No, Rick. This is a philosophical problem, not a financial one."

Rick grimaced. "Is this my fault?"

"Certainly not. Andy and I have been drifting for quite a while. He's changed. He's worried about something, I guess. I can't seem to communicate with him any more. Look, I know he's your best friend, but I'd rather just keep this businesslike. I expect you to charge full commission."

Rick reached for his antacid tablets and popped one in his mouth while his mind raced.

"Night Sky is privately held, Diane. I think it might be hard to place."

"It must be worth something," Diane said with a desperate edge in her voice.

Rick recognized the tone and instantly dropped his voice into consulting mode. "To be quite honest, the first step in cases like this is to approach the majority shareholder. Andy owns the other ninety percent."

"He didn't take the news very well, Rick. I don't think you'll find him cooperative."

Rick sighed. "Do you mind if I talk to him?"

"No, I don't mind. If this is a big problem for you, I could deal with a junior associate."

"No problem, Diane. Leave it with me. I'll get you top dollar, by hook or by crook."

"That sounds better."

"You caught me by surprise, I must say."

"We had a blowout. I guess you figured that much. I really don't know what he's thinking. He's been acting very erratic. In fact, he's off Earthside now, right in the middle of everything. His secretary's starting to panic already.

"Hello, Mister Riley. How's my prize catch today?"

Harlin looked up in surprise from the computer terminal in his room. There could be no mistaking the person before him.

"My name's Sylvia Chiminskaya. I'm the Commander of this vessel." She offered an outstretched hand.

Harlin gaped, unmoving, his mind running old newsreels in memory.

"Are you all right now, Mr. Riley?" The Commander asked again, her arm still out, waiting.

"I'm fine now, sir. Thank you," Harlin said as he reached up to shake her hand. "...for everything, I mean." Impeccably dressed in Space Navy black, the Commander fit Harlin's preconception perfectly, though he was surprised that her femininity showed through the regimental exterior. She had the hourglass figure of a much younger woman, and a fair and delicate face. Tall and solidly built, she cast a domineering presence that demanded respect. Harlin noted her Soviet Space pin, her two Platinum Crosses.

"Sorry I haven't been in to see you earlier. The biomeds told me you needed some rest and I had to get my ship in some semblance of orbit. We're setting up a slight elliptic to minimize the supply runs to Luna. You threw us a bit off schedule, and our computers have been crunching ever since. Anyway, I just wanted to welcome you aboard and offer you the run of the ship. Strategic Metals has offered a pirate's reward for your safe passage."

"Thank you, sir. Sorry to cause you such trouble."

"Trouble. Are you kidding? You're the best thing that's happened to this mission yet—and I don't mean just the publicity down the gravity well. It's a source of personal pride to me the way the crew has rallied around your rescue. For the first time it feels like we're functioning as a team, something I had almost despaired of with all the high-priced help on board. I still find myself longing for my days in the Navy. I appreciate good regimen."

"I can understand that," Harlin replied.

Seeing that perhaps he did not share the sentiment, the Commander looked over his shoulder at the computer screen on his desk. "Into our data already, are you? Anything I can help you with?"

Harlin turned, slightly embarrassed. "I was just looking through your library files. I didn't think anyone would mind."

"No problem at all. You'll find few restrictions on the Early Bird computers. What have you got there? Avant-garde English stuff, is it?"

"I was looking for something specific, though it could be under many titles."

"I don't think you'll find the Manual on our general list, Riley."

Harlin gazed up at the Commander in shock.

She smiled to put him at ease. "I heard you were carrying a friend. The medical staff informed me, of course. A benign immaterial presence, they suggested. They don't know what they're dealing with."

"I don't remember telling anyone."

The Commander shrugged. "No secrets under heavy sedation, I guess. The information alters nothing, believe me. I'm somewhat of a student of the sprites myself. I have some scraps of the Manual in my private file. Here." She reached past Harlin to finger the keyboard, typed in a complicated access code. She smelled of soap and roses. "There you go. Not much, but it's taken me a long time to collect it."

Harlin stared at the screen with a feeling of delighted awe. He recognized the first few lines, a classic piece. He scrolled through until he found something new: *The holy sprites are one, and if one then heirs to all eternal.*

"Incredible," he whispered.

"Good choice of words," the Commander replied.

"And you've never accepted a sprite?"

"I've flirted with them. I'm not totally convinced. And of course I have my career."

"Don't wait too long. You can't count on the future out here in the belt. You could die anytime."

The Commander smiled. "And you never will."

Harlin regarded her intently. "Oh, I'll die, all right. There won't always be a beautiful women to rescue me at the last minute. But some part of me will live on with the sprite, some internal essence."

"So the Manual intimates."

Harlin nodded in deference. "As you know."

"We could ask for a more complete explanation of their purpose and methods," the Commander suggested.

"The sprites do seem to have some difficulty translating eternal truths into temporal concepts," Harlin allowed judicially.

"Indeed, which brings into question the reliability of the documents themselves. The accounts are necessarily filtered and colored by human experience, and therefore subject to error, are they not?"

Harlin shook his head. "I don't believe so. I think the sprites were able to control the very thoughts of the receiver during periods of communication, thereby assuring an infallible message."

"Perhaps."

"It stands to reason."

"Human reason?"

"The sprites are certainly able to communicate as much information as they think we need."

The Commander nodded to defuse the argument. "And to leave us continually wanting more," she added.

Harlin turned his attention back to the computer screen. "It's difficult to explain, but the sprite within me bears witness to the Manual in some direct way that bypasses language, by intuition, I suppose."

The Commander considered Harlin thoughtfully for a moment, her dark blue eyes like heat-treated steel, betraying nothing of her inner state.

"Well, feel free to study what's on file here," she said finally with a gracious smile. "I'll see that you get a hardcopy before you go. If you can add anything from memory I'd be glad to have it. I suspect you have a gold mine tucked away up there. And, once again, welcome to the Early Bird. If there's anything I can do to make your stay more comfortable, feel free to ask."

Harlin turned back to the Commander and stared up at her imposing height. "Now that you mention it, I was wondering..."

The Commander cocked her head at him quizzically. "Yes?" she asked.

"I was wondering...perhaps...if you might have lunch with me one day," Harlin asked with difficulty.

"Lunch?" she echoed in surprise.

Sylvia Chiminskaya thought about it briefly, then smiled like an angel.

Exeter stood up on shaky spindles and massaged the implant scar on his forehead with a grimace of pain. He felt awful. The wire always left him this way, weak, irritable, aching in every lobe of his brain, and he thanked the Dragon the aftereffects were only temporary. In view of the vast rewards, his momentary discomfort seemed a small cross to bear, a tiny thorn in his flesh. He shuffled back and forth across his office with a noticeable slouch that had developed in recent years, his spine arching prematurely with age—fifty-two and looking a hump-backed seventy. A wiry tangle of grey hung from his chin as required by the Guild, but he kept his head shaved to draw attention to the status scar on his forehead. His belly was plump, his torso egglike, for he had no trouble subsisting on the triple rations that were his due as Chairman of Central Committee. The spawn of the Dragon deserved only the best. He picked up a plastic bottle from a wall holder and squeezed a stream of distilled water down his throat. He sighed and licked his lips. All was well at the top of the ladder.

He stabbed the intercom on his desk. "Has Morvick arrived yet?" he asked in his gruff and gravelly baritone.

"No, sir," came the quick reply. "It's two minutes past thirteen."

A good sign, the Chairman considered as he switched off. Morvick's tardiness showed that he was his own man, not some young errand boy pandering for everyone's approval. On the other hand, respect for authority was a valued quality, and a summons from Central Authority was of grave importance. About five minutes late would be optimum, Exeter decided as he settled behind his desk.

Morvick arrived at precisely thirteen-o-five, an accomplished student of procedural politics, and gave the standard palms-up signal of peace.

"Ra lives, Father," he intoned, and took a seat across from the Chairman. Both men wore the distinctive crimson robe of the Ra Guild, complete with purple sash and silver-colored belt at the waist. The Chairman wore a special gold medallion around his neck, indicative of his high office.

"You can call me Exeter, Morvick. This is an informal meeting."

Morvick sat up straighter in his chair, instantly wary. Without the comfort of formality, anything could happen.

"We won't bother with the preliminary jousting of a Committee meeting, Morvick. We're both busy men, so let's get right to the point, shall we? I want to discuss the Dragon's plan for Ceres and your place in the grand scheme of things. What do you personally feel are the Dragon's most important goals?"

Morvick barely suppressed a wince at such a wide open invitation to trouble. His blood told him to run, but his heart said stand firm. He cleared his throat.

"None of us are as close to Ra as we'd like to be. Certainly none with so intimate a relationship as the Chairman of Central Committee."

"Come, come, Morvick, we're outside a Committee meeting now. Indeed why do we bother with all the flimflam? What is the Guild's ultimate purpose?"

Purpose? Goals? "Why—uh—peace and harmony and the general betterment of the colony condition." The standard phrases rolled off Morvick's tongue like well-oiled pebbles.

"Peace and harmony. Yes, yes, you're quite right." Exeter was disappointed and made no effort to conceal it. Perhaps he had expected too much. He settled back in his chair and folded his hands over his rotund belly. "Ra owns everything, you understand. He exists from the beginning of time. And forsaking vaster regions he has chosen Ceres for his personal domain. What humility, what largesse, and yet even here his authority has been usurped. He has been stripped from his rightful place and he wants his glory returned."

Morvick stared dumbfounded, too astonished to understand.

Exeter shook his head as though dealing with a dimwitted child. He leaned forward with artful menace. "Who plunders the precious treasures of his planet and pays him back with water rations and garden seed? Who dictates what his chosen representatives can do and what resources are at their command?"

"Transolar?" Morvick responded.

Exeter smiled and leaned back in his chair once again. "The time has come to throw off the yoke of our oppressors."

Morvick's mind reeled. Transolar was their lifeline to Earth, their source of food, security. "But there are legal contracts and mining agreements," he stammered.

"Bah! Do you think the Dragon cares about useless papers on planets far off in space? Do you think Earth will not buy metals from the Ra Guild as quickly as they do from Transolar? Do you dare to resist the Dragon's will?"

"Certainly not, Chairman," Morvick spit out instantly, struggling to regain his composure. "I was merely pointing out some minor hindrances—naturally the Dragon's will be done. Though I must admit you caught me off guard; I hadn't considered myself important enough to warrant your confidence. Shouldn't a revelation such as this be the subject of a full Committee discussion?"

"The Committee bores me, Morvick. The Fathers could debate about this until Ceres snagged a moon, and still nothing would be done. But we are men of action, you and I. The Dragon has seen your loyalty. He has chosen you to lead your people out of bondage, to make history before the eyes of the solar system. Together we will rule this planet. You will be my chief general. Join with me, and we will make our enemies a footstool for our feet!"

Morvick was stunned. What talk was this? Revolution? Civil war? He fought to control the palpitations in his breast, to halt his body's quick deterioration into panic, and with supreme effort managed to keep a calm and self-assured mask on his face. A critical moment in the game, he knew; do or die, fall or fly. Could it be another test, he wondered. No, the Chairman had gone too far for that.

"The Dragon's will be done," he said smoothly, marveling at himself. "Taking control of the planet will be no small feat though. Public opinion will be crucial, at home as well as on Earth."

"Good. I see you've grasped the situation already. Excellent. You're quite right. These things must be handled delicately. Specifically, we cannot appear as the aggressor. The Ra Guild must be the defender, the protector of human rights and freedoms. If possible, we must appear to come to the rescue of the poor, oppressed masses, to bring peace and justice for all. Don't you agree?"

"Absolutely. But it would seem a difficult assignment."

"On the surface, yes. But as always, Ra provides for his people. The stage is being set even as we talk. The actors are already rehearsing their lines. You've heard of the Fraternity, no doubt."

"The outlaws?"

"Outlaws, yes. Saboteurs, criminals—a loosely organized band of riffraff. Have you never wondered why we delay their extinction?"

Morvick arched his eyebrows in the degree he thought expected. "I had supposed that they were able to conceal themselves in the deep caverns."

"Hah!" Exeter exclaimed, immensely pleased with himself. "Do you think Ra cannot handle a bunch of boys who pretend to be men? Perhaps they can elude the Transolar Security police, but never the Ra Guild. No, Morvick, the Dragon allows the rebels to survive in order to suit his own designs. We play them like a well-tuned instrument, like puppets dancing on a string. Now their time has come."

Morvick felt an electric chill shiver through his body. He was caught in something bigger than he could ever have imagined. He smiled at Exeter and nodded, not trusting himself to speak.

"Let us assume for the sake of discussion," the Chairman began confidently, "that the Fraternity's complaints and concerns are legitimate, or at least were made to appear legitimate—they have no water, you understand, a fact that works in our favor. Suppose a small but vocal minority took up arms in violent protest. How hard do you think it would be for the Ra Guild to swing public opinion in favor of the rebellion? A sermon here, a carefully worded proclamation there—I imagine it could be done."

"But Transolar would wipe out the uprising at the first sign of trouble," Morvick exclaimed. "It would be a massacre."

"Exactly. Picture the newsfax headlines Earthside: Heartless corporate henchmen murder servile native miners. Riot police kill hundreds on Ceres. In that type of situation, who could blame the Ra Guild for stepping in to maintain order amid the chaos?" The Chairman folded his hands in front of him with dramatic innocence.

Morvick had to smile in the face of such perfection, to see Ra's will in such simple beauty. He began to chuckle as harbored tension found release, and Exeter joined in the merriment with him. How easy it would be if all went according to plan. Like young boys sharing a secret joke, the two politicians sat laughing together.

Morvick had reached the end of his long ambitious journey. The pinnacle of power awaited him now. For years he had longed to be a part of the Guild's upper echelon, to be a member of the small clique that shaped society, and suddenly here it was within reach, so easily grasped, a gift from the gods. Could he possibly refuse such an offer?

"How soon?" he asked as the laughter dissipated.

"A few weeks," Exeter told him, serious once again. "I have information that the Fraternity is planning a major attack on the spaceport. We'll make our move then."

"You have an informant in the Fraternity?"

Exeter smiled in affirmation. "The eyes of Ra are everywhere."

"Long live the Dragon."

"And long may the Guild reign," the Chairman added. "We'll need a small armed regiment, fifty or sixty trustworthy men. My secretary Lamarr has some names lined up. I'll secure the laser pistols. The propaganda will have to be handled carefully; we don't want to alarm Transolar with anything overt. Subtle and surreptitious at first, we'll lead the lambs along slowly and build them up to a crescendo. By the time we're finished, every mother on Ceres will cringe to think that Transolar might exploit her baby, and every father will pound his fist on the table in support of the Fraternity. We'll keep our strategy to ourselves until I decide who else might prove useful in the new regime. Agreed?"

"Don't you trust the other Ra Fathers?"

"A few perhaps. Some are more useful than others. We'll see who needs to know as things progress."

Morvick eyed Exeter critically. Was he close enough now to broach the unnameable? To loose his heartstrings?"

"Was it because of my daughter that I was chosen?" he asked quietly.

"That may have been a factor, yes," Exeter replied evenly. "Do you think Ra tests you too hard?"

Morvick met the Chairman's gaze and hesitated. "I find it difficult," he confessed.

Exeter darted his eyes to the desk in front of him. He rubbed his implant scar with a nervous right hand. "My own daughter was a sacrifice many years ago, Morvick," he said. He looked up. "The memory passes quickly, believe me."

The two men lapsed silent as each examined his private pain, Morvick's fresh and vivid like an open gash, Exeter's old and nagging like a wound that never healed properly. Ra chose his leaders carefully. He made no mistakes. Those who would serve the Dragon must do so totally, with undivided attention and uncompromising loyalty. He was not a god to be trifled with. As metal tried in a furnace of fire, he purified his servants, separating the silver from the dross. He loved to watch them squirm under his heavy hand.

"We'll have to do away with these terrible beards in the new order," Exeter said to banish the melancholy mood. "I've never understood why we wear them." He scratched the grey tangle at his throat.

"I had always assumed it was a part of Ra's will," Morvick replied with a shrug.

Exeter shook his head. "It's amazing what gets attributed to a god over the years," he muttered.

"I suppose so."

"And we won't have any more nonsense about celibacy for the Ra Fathers—it takes too much of the sweetness out of ordination. I've got my eye on one young mother already." He chuckled. "No more creeping in the shadows. We'll be able to start fresh—a new spool on the history tapes."

"It will be a great day for Ceres," said Morvick.

"A great day," Exeter agreed. "But until then we've got to watch our step. If Transolar ever got wind of our plan, they'd have a whole battalion of Security police on the next freighter. It will be difficult enough as it is. I just hope the Fraternity can muster up enough of a battle to make our response look plausible. We'll have to make sure they're well armed."

"The Dragon's will be done," Morvick repeated.

"And we've got to keep corporate relations running smoothly until the right moment. Those smoke-eaters aren't as stupid as they look, you know. Which reminds me—I've got a memo here from Transolar." Exeter opened a desk drawer and shuffled some papers around. "Right, here it is—an asteroid miner is due to be dropped off by some sort of traveling space laboratory, and Transolar wants us to provide first-class accommodation for the fellow until he can get a berth to Luna City. He could be a spy—I wouldn't put it past them. You'll have to take care of it personally, Morvick. Can I count on you?" he asked as he handed the memo over.

"No problem, Exeter."

"See that everything looks normal and make sure that no one from the Fraternity gets near him. A celebrity like this could be a target for them—a possible hostage. I can control the Fraternity to a great extent, but you never know when some wild-eyed romantic is going to run off half-cocked on his own. We can't afford anything embarrassing at this point."

"I'll keep him out of trouble."

"Your loyalty has been proven time and time again. You will be amply rewarded in the new world."

"To serve Ra is its own reward," Morvick answered dutifully.

"That's the spirit. I can see we're off to a famous start. I'm sure the Prime Minister's chair will be the perfect spot for you. We'll arrange an election with all the requisite fanfare. How does that sound?"

"Very good, Exeter." Prime Minister Morvick Zacheus—he tested the name like a bite of sacred meat on his palate.

"Fine. It's all settled then. See my secretary Lamarr for all the bothersome details and keep me informed of your progress. I'll want a full report within a week. I should have the Fraternity's final timetable by then. We've got to play our hand carefully, Morvick. Timing will be critical. It's taken a lot of ground work to arrange this opportunity. Let's not waste it."

"I'll be careful."

"Good. Ra lives." Chairman Englehart stood and gave the standard signal, hand raised to face level with palm outward.

"Ra lives," Morvick countered.

After they had touched palms briefly in ceremonial salute, Morvick left the Chairman alone in his office. In a few seconds Exeter Englehart was back under the wire.

The mountains were old and tired, their sharp peaks rounded by eons of wind and rain, like ancient warriors now bowing in submission to the elements. A cotton-ball covering of vegetation clung to their gentle-curves—a fluffy mauve blanket of trees silencing the dark earth below. The occasional spruce top speared through the froth with a dark green spire like a giant arrow pointing to the heavens, but the majority of the forest stood skeletal in the early spring season. Close inspection revealed the swollen red buds on the branches, promising the age-old renewal of winter into spring, the primal heat coaxing life from cold dormancy, the hills slowly being reborn, the face of the land quietly being transformed by the miracle of re-creation.

The poplar trees, ugly in their old age with gnarled and grotesque, sickly yellow limbs, were first off the mark in the race for the seasonal sun. Their buds had already burst into tiny, pale green leaves, so that the lowland areas where they congregated already showed a faint tinge of life, the light green color standing in sharp contrast to the overall purple hue of the hills. The sky was clear of clouds, a crisp and clean and perfect azure;

the ground predominantly dry, though odd patches of snow still nestled deep in the shadows of the forest like wounded comrades left behind on a battlefield lost.

It had taken Andy McKay most of the morning to reach his pinnacle vantage point. Now perched on a rock shelf high above a cobalt-blue lake, he drank in the panorama like a man thirsty for water, a man long dry in the desert of space. Dark green coniferous forest circled the lake as round an oasis, spruce and cedar soaking up the fecund swampland. And where the rocky slope rose sharply from the water, the long-needled pines had made their purchase, every nook and fracture crammed with eager roots. They grew miraculously out of sheer rock faces, hanging precariously to each tiny crevice, and yet the stormiest gale could not dislodge their firm anchors.

Andy spotted his lone canoe on the shore far below, a tiny sliver of white plastiglass starkly out of place in the wild, an encroachment, a transgression. He wondered if ever a man had stood on this precipice and witnessed this scene. He felt like a primitive explorer on an unnamed and uncharted land, an eager bridegroom for the first time viewing his beloved virgin's hidden delights.

The wind coaxed a somber symphony from the forest, a whisper, a gentle caress. Without beginning or end, without birth or decay, the breath of life rounded the horizon like a runner rejoicing in the movement of sinew and muscle. To Andy the wind was a rejuvenating tonic. He'd spent too many years breathing the sterile gases of space—computer-controlled, canned atmosphere, always optimum in temperature and humidity but suffocatingly stale in comparison to the wild winds of Earth.

"Why have you brought me here?" he asked the unseen guardian that had hounded him for weeks. "What do you want from me?" he shouted into the rising wind in vain. He felt like a fool, like a bug on a vast plain of existence. He was the trespasser here, the alien in a strange and unknown terrain. In his rush for a career in space, in his longing for financial success, he had forgotten his birthplace and had divorced himself from all natural thought and action. He dropped to his knees and pressed his bearded cheek on the sun-warmed bedrock. He closed his eyes as the whistling wind stroked his face, teased his eyelashes and tousled his ragged red hair. He searched for a prayer, an anthem of grace to still his anxious heart.

How long had he been wandering in this wilderness, he wondered. Nine cycles? Ten? All the days seemed to run together in his mind, the threads of time tangled like gossamer filaments. He had scoffed at the survival training offered by the wilderness rangers, and had picked his own route oblivious to their warnings. Had he not navigated to the moon and back a hundred times through the icy vacuum of space? Had he not proved his courage, his stamina, his determination a thousand times? What challenge could this old mother planet offer him now? What danger?

Hypothermia, the rangers insisted, the slow sleep of death. The ice was barely gone and the water remained frigid, as if reluctantly accepting the change of season, refusing to awaken from the slumber of winter freeze. A man awash might have only minutes to save himself, and how gentle the slide into cold comfort, how inviting the last relaxation. Alone a man gives up quickly, he closes his eyes.

But Andy clung to his righteous pride and demanded admittance to the wildest northern regions. He wanted to find a land pure and free and clean, untrammeled by featherless bipeds. With smug confidence he waved goodbye to the seaplane pilot who deposited him at his prearranged starting point. He looked up at gathering clouds with a grin, and a cold rain quickly washed the smile from his face.

At first he reveled in the fresh water from the sky, letting it soak into his hair and pour down into his open mouth, for water was scarce in space, conserved and recycled, tasteless and tepid; but the rain continued day after day in a slow, clammy drizzle, gradually seeping everywhere and soaking everything, blurring the passing of time itself as the careful chronological boundaries of eating and sleeping were marred, misplaced in a grey void. Lighting a fire quickly became next to impossible, and grubbing for dry wood in the forest a time-consuming task. In the mornings Andy covered runny stools with soggy leaves and nibbled biscuit from his rations; in the evenings he shivered in front of a meager, sputtering fire and tried to boil a sip of tea to warm his aching bones. At night he dreamed of metal monsters clawing the sky far above him, spitting a white mist of nuclear plasma.

Water and fire, water and fire, and at dawn, before the rising of the sun, the unseen guardian woke Andy with a gentle call. Somewhere between sleep and wakefulness, it demanded his attention, it pricked and prodded at his weak spots. Some mornings he felt he was going mad, a schizoid self slowly emerging. Other mornings he responded as to an old friend, and that scared him worst of all. What exactly is a thought, Andy considered. A burst of electrical activity in the brain? A chemical reaction? What communication could there be without language, without patterns of mutual recognition? Water and fire, and nowhere left to run.

Even now, atop his ancient mountain peak, Andy felt a nagging mental unease that kept him from relaxing. He shrugged off his meditations and stood to his feet, eyeing the sun in the latter half of its arc. A pilgrim must keep moving while daylight lingers, he told himself. In darkness and ignorance no man can work.

He checked his map against the wide panorama below him, trying to match landmarks to colored squiggles on paper. He made a few notations on the map with a felt-tipped marker, and, satisfied, began a halting journey back down the rocky incline. Occasionally the path became too steep, forcing him to double back and try another route, but for the most part his way was unhindered, the rocks dry, the moss and lichen spongy under his feet. He had budgeted his time wisely and had no need to hurry. He breathed deep of life.

Near the base of the mountain, he came upon a wild jumble of sharp-edged boulders leaning crazily on each other. Piled helter-skelter by a cruel gravity, they looked like discarded potsherds of a giant potter, broken toys left strewn. Andy mentally tried to piece the rocks back into the cliff face high above; this one fit here, turned just so, that one just underneath. He tried to imagine them as they fell crashing to the ground, laying waste everything in their path, mowing down huge timbers like matchsticks in great clouds of dust and debris. As he investigated further, he noticed a tiny mountain stream etching the rock face above, and he realized with a start that the tiny trickle of water over the years had cut the boulders loose like a knife through wax.

By the time Andy reached his campsite on the shore, the frogs were announcing the encroaching evening, their eery chirruping chorus echoing around the lake, a rhythmic and strangely beautiful serenade. As darkness pulled a cloak around him, it occurred to Andy that he might never hear this wild symphony again, not this song, not this particular verse. A loon cried far off in the distance as if to punctuate the thought, and the evening became suddenly unique and precious to the wandering millionaire from space. Each day is precious, he considered, and he had wasted so many.

Andy gazed up at the stars to let familiar friends and well-known constellations comfort him. The night sky was his home, the one stable reference around which he had structured his life. There was order in the universe, mathematical precision to which he could relate. Astrophysics and celestial navigation were religious doctrines to him, foundations for his mental and spiritual experience. Such incredible sophistication, such miraculous complexity. Was there indeed a creator god maintaining this masterpiece? Could it possibly be the chance outcome of conflict and competition, of an unknowable explosion at the beginning of time, subatomic particles colliding at random to produce such perfection?

He looked up at the rising moon and longed for Diane. She had been with him for years, partner and mistress, and now had chosen to walk out of his life forever. She could have any man she wanted, he knew. She had the smarts, the classic beauty. What did she want from life? A career? Money? Power? Children? Why had he never asked her before? Was their relationship so superficial that he didn't know her heart's desire? Was this called love—this ache in his diaphragm, this pain?

"Can you get her back for me?" he asked the unseen guardian, and as the words left his lips he felt a pure conviction deep in his soul, a perfect justice so mysterious and ineffable that its presence brought tears to his eyes. He saw a flash of lightning far off on the horizon and felt the first few drops of rain on his face before the low rumble of thunder reached his ears, and he knew that nothing would ever be the same again. And as his heavy tears coursed down his dirty face and dripped from the thick stubble on his chin, the wind-stroked trees clapped their boughs in applause, the mighty mountains echoed with solemn approval, and all the angels shouted for joy.

PART THREE

"Ever been to Ceres before, sir?"

The shuttle pilot was a stubby young man with a basketball belly. He was neatly dressed, his uniform clean and wrinkle-free, but his stringy black hair was unkempt and a little longer than Early Bird regulations allowed. He would be on report soon if he didn't get it cut.

"No, I haven't," Harlin answered. Eros, Deimos, he added privately, but never a closed shop like Ceres.

"Here, have a cigar." The pilot offered an ugly brown roll of tobacco.

"Thanks, I don't smoke."

"Take it; you'll need it anyway," the fat man persisted with a smile. His teeth were yellow and crooked.

"What for?"

"It'll hide the smell. Just carry it like a stick of incense. Everyone does."

Harlin eyed the cigar doubtfully.

"There's no water," the pilot explained. "The natives can't wash. You'll be glad of the cigar, believe me."

"I'll be all right, thanks."

Harlin nodded to dismiss the conversation, but inwardly he winced at what lay ahead. He remembered with displeasure the stale air on Eros—and that had been only a few thousand miners, a bare skeleton crew when compared to a thriving colony. He should have signed on with the Early Bird, he told himself. He belonged on the frontier with the other spacers—perhaps out on Ganymede where life was cheap and the pay exorbitant. There was nothing for him on Luna or even Earth. No one awaited his return. His parents were dead, his mother on life-support in an organ morgue, her "dignity of death" preserved while surgeons plucked body parts one by one for transplant. Two brothers and one sister had disowned him when he accepted his sprite. Sylvia had understood. Harlin had felt the mutual attraction between them, the natural magnetic. They might have developed something together, something worth keeping forever.

"Okay, sir," the pilot replied with a shrug. "Don't say I didn't warn you," he added with a knowing smile.

"Why do you keep calling me sir?" Harlin demanded. "I don't outrank you. I'm just a civilian."

"Oh, sorry, sir. Just habit, I guess. What with you being so chummy with the Commander and all, I just figured..."

"I'm just a spider miner. It takes more nerve than skill. Commander Chiminskaya and I merely happened to have a few things in common to talk about, that's all."

"Interesting that you should say that, sir. We noticed—the boys and I—that you and the Commander didn't—ah—you were never seen in her quarters, I mean."

"Of course not."

"I suppose you must have made alternate arrangements—given the delicacy of the situation."

77

"Just what are you driving at, mister?"

The pilot chuckled with false ease. "Well, you know how it is on these long voyages."

Sure, Harlin nodded, three stars for performing in the Commander's bed, instant status shipwide. He was beginning to get irritated with this slovenly-looking man.

"It's just a little bet the boys and I have going. We were hoping you might help us out." The fat man tried to smile, but it was a forced caricature.

Harlin didn't return the effort. "Do you want specifics or just a simple yes or no?"

The pilot guffawed with an overly loud release of tension. "Hah, I knew it! Those straight-laced types let loose like gangbusters, right?"

"What was your name again?" Harlin asked.

"Sullivan," the pilot answered with a yellow smile.

"Well, Sullivan, I hope you're honest enough to pay off your bets promptly."

The smile faded. "Eh?"

"Commander Chiminskaya runs a disciplined ship, mister. She hasn't got time for personal frivolity."

The fat man clamped his lips shut. His face darkened a bright crimson.

"Don't worry," Harlin added, "I won't let word of your gambling get back to her ears."

Harlin dismissed the conversation by turning to look out the porthole at Ceres, a pitted spheroid just under five hundred miles in diameter. With no atmosphere to smooth the sharp edges and no dust to fill the tiny crevices, the coal-black exterior appeared as rough as a grinding wheel. The spaceport, shining like a lighthouse, offered the only evidence of colonization below the surface. Harlin was reminded of a one-eyed mythical beast.

Little gravity down there, Harlin considered, just those magnetic slippers supplied by Transolar to keep your feet on the ground. No actual bodily stability, no comforting pressure on your soles. Harlin had never liked living underground, not even on luxurious Luna. The endless tunnels made him feel caged like a rat, lost in a maze. On Ceres it could only be worse. No water, the pilot had said. Strict rations, probably dehydration. Harlin sighed to himself. He hoped the inside esthetic was nicer than this ugly view from above. Just a rough-hewn chunk of black rock, Ceres looked like the type of planet that would have a funeral dirge for a national anthem.

Sullivan muttered quietly to his control panel as he made final corrections and fired his retros, and a muffled roar shook the tiny craft as it decelerated for touchdown. On the planet below, huge doors of reinforced spacesteel slid back into the ground like huge eyelids exposing a giant eyeball—the docking pads empty except for a few small shuttlecraft and geological scanners, all with Transolar insignias on their sides. Harlin sighed again at the absence of a Space Navy freighter.

The shuttle bumped down with barely a tremor. Sullivan winked and Harlin nodded in compliment.

"You'll have to suit up to get inside, sir. I'm not equipped to match up with a Transolar lock. You sure you don't want to take a cigar along? Everyone usually does."

"I'll have to get used to the smell sometime. It looks like I'm stuck here for awhile."

"I wasn't supposed to say anything, but the Commander told me to bring you back if you changed your mind."

Harlin eyed the man thoughtfully. Sylvia said that? She must have known he wouldn't change his mind on a whim; he was still under contract to Strategic Metals. He nodded. "Tell her I'll be looking for her when the sprites gather."

The pilot gaped after Harlin as the latter donned his spacesuit and airlocked out. He had never met a sprite carrier in person, and had thought the cult had been eradicated along with the old religions of Earth many years ago. Surely the Commander couldn't be involved in something like that, he wondered.

The feeling came back to Harlin as he walked across the tarmac—that claustrophobic panic he'd had those last few hours in his spider, his heartbeat heavy in his ears, his breathing hoarse and oppressive, a band of aching steel around his chest as he struggled to pull in nonexistent oxygen. He fought back the urge to run.

"I've had it now," he told his inoperative suit radio, hoping his own voice would help calm him. "Space has finally got to me. I'm no good for anything any more. A simple vacuum walk and my nerves are jangling like a red alert in an overheated engine room. This must be what it's like to go space crazy."

He imagined Ceres a living entity under his feet, a hungry cyclops ready to swallow him like an insect.

"Paranoia," he whispered to himself. "Easy, Harlin," he coaxed, "let your sprite carry you through the bad parts."

When the underground airlock flashed green he stepped into a large locker room and quickly unclipped his helmet. The stench assaulted him like a physical blow—a heavy, dirty, subhuman smell mingled with the chemical undertones of powerful disinfectant. He gagged, held his breath for several seconds, and with deliberate effort tried another shallow sip of air. He could never get used to this, he told himself, cursing his foul luck.

He climbed out of his spacesuit and stowed it in the airlock for ground crew to deliver back to the shuttle. He pulled a pair of magnetic slippers from a dispenser on the wall and snapped them on over his jumpsuit boots. He tested them on the treadway. A slight jump and he was airborne, had probably even reached escape velocity, he considered. He pushed back off the low ceiling and stuck to the floor. Keep one foot on the ground or fly free, he decided. No freighter on the dock, no gravity. From bad to worse, he told himself, wondering what in space he was doing here.

In the main reception area Harlin found two guards standing idly with holstered laser pistols on their belts and bright red insignias on their beige coveralls. Transolar Security, he noted, muscular giants imported from Earth, probably on short duration to preserve bodily strength and keep their bones from cracking upon transfer to a gravity assignment.

"Riley?" grunted one man, and glanced at a digital readout on the wall. He made a notation on a computer keypad and flipped open a small communications module on his wrist. "Is the Ra Guild sending someone up for this spider miner?" he asked.

Behind him, an airlock slid open to reveal a lanky man in a dark crimson robe.

"Never mind," he said. "An escort just arrived." He dropped his wrist as Morvick Zacheus skated forward.

"Sorry I'm late, Mr. Riley," the Ra Father said, slightly out of breath from exertion. His face was almost obscured by the grey tangle of long hair and beard, but his beady black eyes seemed animate and intelligent to Harlin. A purple sash was draped over his right shoulder and pinned together on his left side. A silver belt circled his waist. Magnetic weights in the hem of his garment kept it sweeping the floor as he moved, and the pendulum action made it ripple as though blown by variable winds. Even after he came to a stop in front of Harlin, his robe continued to move with a life of its own.

"Welcome to Ceres. My name is Morvick Zacheus."

"A pleasure," Harlin lied, and extended his hand.

Morvick grasped Harlin's hand and shook it heartily. "It is an honor to meet you, good friend. I understand you are a man of some stature. A mining specialist?"

"I guess you could say that." Harlin allowed himself to be led past the two Security guards. "Have you heard of spider mining?"

"No, I'm afraid you'll have to tell me all about it. You'll be staying in my own home. We'll have time to talk."

"Do you have any idea when the next freighter is due?"

"We're approaching one of our best windows in about fifteen days," Morvick replied. "We'll be getting freighters weekly for about a month after that. You picked a good time for a quick transfer."

Fifteen days. Harlin groaned inwardly. Fifteen days on bread and water and foul air. He should have signed on with the Early Bird, he told himself again. Full centrifugal gravity, good food, a pleasant companion, perhaps a new career. Instead he was trapped on a sterile rock with stick-figure corporate slaves. What bizarre sense of duty had brought him here?

Harlin watched Morvick carefully as he followed the elder man on a tour of some of the farms—spacious tunnels of leafy green, with plants growing inward from all surfaces toward a central glowlight. His host pointed out the hydroponic pumps like a schoolboy giving a demonstration, and though well acquainted with colonial agriculture, Harlin couldn't help but play the part of the sightseeing tourist in the face of Morvick's obvious pride. He wondered how Morvick could be content in such an austere environment, and found himself liking the man despite everything. He was born here, Harlin reminded himself. In his own home a man finds peace in any circumstance.

Yet Morvick seemed nervous and guarded for some reason, as though rehearsing everything he said before he opened his mouth. Harlin supposed it was out of deference to his position as a spider miner, having observed the special status afforded him by those outside his profession. Miners ultimately paid the bills in the asteroid belt. Research is nice, and higher learning grand, but man never would have climbed out of Earth's gravity well without money in his pocket.

"What's your occupation, Morvick? That ceremonial robe you're wearing looks like a judge's garb."

"Actually I'm a priest. We look after most of the day-to-day affairs on Ceres."

"A priest." Harlin's curiosity was instantly aroused—a priest, right out in the open and completely legal. "That's interesting. Do you follow the Manual?"

"No, no, we have nothing to do with any occult literature," Morvick replied good-naturedly. "We follow Ra the Dragon, a major celestial deity."

Harlin felt his sprite twitch within him, a sensation almost of pain. Harlin tightened his abdomen in response, suddenly unsure of himself. "A dragon?" he said.

Morvick laughed. "Don't look so worried. He's really a kindhearted and generous beast. He provides all these magnificent gardens and the very air we breathe, asking only for the adoration of his people in return. Naturally I can't expect you to understand everything at once, but you'll learn more as your stay progresses. I suppose you hold to one of the old gods of Earth, do you?"

"I belong to the sprites who created the universe."

Morvick's jaw dropped. "The universe? All the stars and planets?"

"That seems to be the plain teaching of the Manual."

"You mean to say these sprites claim the whole universe as their domain? What manner of beings are they?"

"I'm not sure. Apparently the universe that we know represents only a small fraction of their total reality."

"Impossible," Morvick exclaimed, then quickly mastering himself added, "meaning no disrespect, of course."

Harlin smiled. "None taken. The truth is that I believe in something that is not easily translated into language, that is in fact supernatural, so I'm at somewhat of a disadvantage in debate."

"I can see the problem," Morvick agreed, nodding, and lapsed into silence.

What conversation that later arose became strangely stilted after religious views had been aired. It seemed to the two men that their respective gods were incompatible, perhaps even at odds. Each had the wary feeling that the other's philosophy was unreliable, that the other had somehow been deceived. They talked uncomfortably of other things as Morvick showed the spider miner to his quarters. A sick daughter, Marinda, slept next door, Morvick warned, and asked that she not be disturbed.

Time schedules had not matched up well for Harlin. Somehow he had missed a night's sleep in the shuffle from the Early Bird to Ceres. As he allowed himself to relax he noticed a heaviness at the back of his skull, a groggy feeling as though his head was filled with foam rubber. The bed in his room was twice the size of the tiny cots on the spaceship. He tested the mattress—a firm, air cushion with elastic straps at the sides to prevent airborne injury during sleep. Harlin grimaced at the prospect of low-g nightmares again, but resigned himself to his situation. He was too tired to worry at the moment. He was stuck here for fifteen days at least. He longed for deep and dreamless sleep.

Harlin pulled off his magnetic slippers and, not bothering to undress further, pulled a rough blanket up over his head and closed his eyes. Sleep hovered just inches away, tantalizingly close. He could feel her reaching for him with gentle fingers, promising solace, coaxing him away from his problems like a warm and winsome woman.

A tortured scream shattered the silence, jolting Harlin upright like an electric shock. His pulse raced. His muscles tensed like wire drawn taut.

He heard weeping in the next room. Morvick's sick daughter. He heard Morvick's footsteps sweep by outside his door. Another scream sounded, a terror pure and atavistic. Harlin jerked out of bed and careened off the wall and across the room before gaining his balance.

He heard Morvick's voice in the next room, cooing and warbling against a background of muffled argument. Harlin pulled himself into the hallway and along the rough wall hand over hand. He peeked into the next room to see Marinda bound and gagged in a chair, and her father stabbing a syringe into her writhing shoulder. Harlin pulled back and swallowed his fear. He felt like a predator, a voyeur. He quickly pushed off and sailed back to his own room, caught the doorframe and dragged himself inside. He tangled himself back into his cot just as Morvick skated by outside and peered in at him. He feigned sleep as his heart pounded with anxiety.

Tova looked like a starving man, his cheeks hollow, his lips stretched tightly over his teeth, his beard sparse and stringy like wisps of black smoke clinging to his chin. He was thin and frail-boned like a bird, but not for lack of food—he burned up his allotted calories like a furnace hungry for fuel, his young metabolism racing, churning at stress pitch, his mind always scheming, dreaming, always worried about the Fraternity. The responsibility lay with him. He was the leader.

He could hear the brothers now, the sound of their mingled voices echoing up from the serpentine tunnels below—voices eager with anticipation, brimming with the excitement of soldiers whose moment of glory was still distant enough to be out of focus, not yet replaced with the somber mood of those for whom the battle was only minutes away.

Deliberately noiseless, Tova eased his way inside the bubble-shaped cavity and clung to the ceiling like a spider. He counted thirty-five men below in the meager light—all the cell leaders from this area, a perfect turnout. Tova smiled with grim satisfaction. The warriors were ready for the culmination.

"You make more noise than school boys," he shouted down to the young men. "Shall Security advance on you as easily as I?"

The soldiers looked at each other sheepishly, their exuberance having got the better of them. No one offered a response to the legendary figure above them—no excuses, no explanation.

Tova pushed himself off the ceiling and fell in gentle slow motion, his large canvas bag trailing behind him like a balloon on a string. He landed softly and silently, dropping to a crouch to cushion his inertia.

"Never mind; the tunnels are empty above," he told the assembled group. "How go the preparations in these sectors?"

A tall and unusually stocky man with a shock of blond hair drooping on his forehead spoke up, "Everything is green, Tova. Do you bring the final schedule?"

"Are you the elected representative, Drako?"

"I am."

"So be it. You have six cycles, lieutenant, then the spaceport will be ours. But more than schedules, I bring you guns." Tova flung his canvas bag at the feet of the newly commissioned officer. Laser pistols spilled out into the air, spinning and dancing like children's jacks—brand-new weapons with red Transolar insignias embossed neatly on the sides.

Drako caught a pistol as it bounced up to him and eyed it approvingly, pushing the wavy hair from his eyes with his left hand. "We sting the viper with his own poison, eh? No wonder you are the leader and we the followers." He smiled as the brothers scrambled to corral the floating weapons.

Tova allowed himself a brief chuckle. "A greater force leads us all, lieutenant. We all have tasks according to our abilities. You and your people have your assignments memorized, I trust." It could have been a query, had there been any room for imperfection in Tova's mind.

"We have the Security barracks in Sector Thirty-Seven and the communication tower in Sector Seventeen," Drako rattled off, "the tower to be secured and the barracks bottled up. We've over a hundred and fifty men ready to go."

"Excellent."

"If you don't mind me saying so, sir," Drako continued with some hesitance, "the men have wondered why the barracks personnel cannot be eliminated, perhaps quietly gassed."

Tova nodded as though in agreement, or at least understanding, then leveled a gaze on his lieutenant and spoke firmly so that all might hear. "There is more to be considered in this operation than simple revenge, my friend. Security staff will be detained until you hear the retreat code from me or one of my generals. We will brook no divergence from the master plan."

Drako bowed in deference. He understood that it was not the lieutenant's place to know every detail of the master plan, just as a servant need not understand the will of his master. The servant need only obey the master and emulate him in all his ways. "As you say," he answered. "I promised the men a hearing, is all."

"You've had it, lieutenant. You will be given the cease-fire password on the Day, and may appoint one other as second in command to receive the signal and act upon it in the event of your death—crimson secret otherwise. Do you foresee any problems with the Security barracks?"

"None, commander. We've found a natural rock fault we can blow to block the main tunnel. It will take those smoke-eaters at least two cycles to dig through the rubble. That will leave them only one exit for us to cover with our guns. No one will get through. We should be able to hold such a stalemate indefinitely with a minimum of bloodshed."

"And you have enough explosives for the job?"

Drako grinned. "More than enough—smuggled off the job site little by little for two years."

Tova nodded curtly without a smile. He swept the congregation with a squinty-eyed stare that each man felt like a cold finger pointing to his heart, reaching for his soul, testing the depths. A great man is known by the size of his dreams, by the strength of ambition. Few men pay heed when the small dreams of a lesser man reach fulfilment, but everyone sees and admires the unreachable heights of a great man's dream. If success smiles, the whole world fawns at the feet of a great man; if he fails he can bear it, for he knows he dreamed a great dream. Good men will follow such a dreamer, thoughtful men will warm to his vision, and brave men will gamble everything for the chance of victory. Standing like an icon, a focus of spiritual energy, Tova mesmerized the brothers with the promise he harbored, the hope that burned inside him like a consuming fire.

The silence lingered claustrophobic, an emotional vacuum, until Tova's rich voice filled the gloom like a chalice overflowing: "Brothers, you hold in your hands the future of Ceres. You hold in your hands the inheritance of your children, of generations yet unborn. We have journeyed a long and dangerous path to reach this place, and many of our friends have been killed along the way. Their blood cries out from the rock for vengeance, urging us on to battle. The time for strategies and tactical debate has come to an end. Now is the hour for the common soldier to prove his worth, the hour of glory. I have been round the globe to meet with your Fraternity brothers as I meet with you now, and have found a strong army of one mind and purpose, of one heritage and one destiny. We all must depend on the men beside us, that the chain might not be broken at its weakest link. That is the message I bring to you today. Your brothers are depending on you. Our entire native race is depending on you. I, Tova, am depending on you. In six cycles the dividing line will be drawn, success or failure, victory or defeat.

"I know, brothers, that our enemy may seem monolithic to you now—the unconquerable Transolar Corporation, owner of half the colonies in the solar system—but let me remind you that the smoke-eaters are but men like us. They thirst for water as we thirst for water, they bleed as we bleed, but they die with but a small fraction of the dignity with which we die. The Security police are mere hirelings, whereas we fight for what rightfully belongs to us. It is true that we cannot gain ultimate control of our planet. Would that it were not so, but you all know as well as I that our colony is not self-sufficient. For the sake of water, we need Transolar more than they need us. But think not that our effort will be wasted. Once we control the broadcast stations, our claims and demands will be transmitted throughout the solar system at the speed of light, and the Earth will shake with the sound thereof. The blow we strike will reverberate for ages to come, and one day—perhaps next week, perhaps next year—Ceres will be free and our children will no longer be slaves to a corporate machine. So put on the armor of self-assurance, brothers, and prepare yourselves for victory, for we will not fail. I have seen the future written on the myriad faces of the Fraternity as I see it on your faces now. Our success is printed there on your foreheads and in your eyes. Look at each other and see. A new day awaits us, a day of brotherly love and equality for all. Long live the Fraternity! Let this be our battle cry."

"Long live the Fraternity!" the brothers repeated in unison, savoring the feel of it on their lips and in their mouths.

"Long live the Fraternity!" they shouted again, and their blood seemed to thicken in their veins at the sound.

Tova raised his hands in benediction. "Every man has his task to perform. Let nothing deter him from his duty. Let each man prepare his heart in his own way. Our children's children will remember our deeds, brothers. I leave the future in your hands. Long live the Fraternity!"

"Long live the Fraternity!" The deep caverns echoed with the thunder of their voices.

Tova greeted each brother personally as the men separated into small groups to rehearse their timetables. He knew each man by name and had recruited a good number of them himself. In each case Tova had the needed words of encouragement, the strong arm to grasp, the silent nod of approval. It satisfied him immensely to talk to these chosen few. Their excitement was electric, their determination contagious. Here was the meaning of life, Tova reflected—to have a cause to fight for, a philosophy to believe in, something to die for. How empty life would be without something worth dying for.

Central Authority was peaceful and quiet, like the frozen stillness before a detonation in the mines. Morvick could feel the tension building at the back of his neck as he walked past vacant Guild offices, his anxiety slowly coiling like a spring under pressure. Exeter's secretary was not at his desk, so Morvick knocked on the

Chairman's door and, hearing the familiar voice inside, let himself in.

"Ra lives, Fa—" He stopped short.

Exeter was reclining in the chair behind his desk, murmuring and moaning as though in great pain, his tongue lolling out the side of his open mouth, his eyes closed—a slack-jawed idiot, oblivious to everything around him.

Startled initially, Morvick felt his face grow hot with embarrassment as he realized his trespass. He had known for years that the Chairman of the Ra Guild was wired for pleasure, but had never before witnessed him under the influence. His curiosity aroused, he moved a few steps closer, a knot of disgust beginning to form in his stomach like a bad nut. A drop of drool slid down the Chairman's chin as the contorted man rocked in his private sea of sensation.

Morvick retreated to the safety of the outer office just as Exeter's secretary returned from his errands. Their eyes met and locked meaningfully, but neither hazarded a word. Lamarr opened a briefcase on his desk and began filing documents. Morvick sat uncomfortably on a white plastiglass chair. Time passed slowly.

"Send Morvick in when he arrives," the intercom rasped.

Morvick jumped to his feet and moved to the door. Lamarr glanced up from his work with a barely perceptible nod.

"Ra lives, Father."

"Ra lives, Morvick." The pale Chairman mopped his face with a towel. "Give me a minute. I've just been under the wire."

Morvick took a seat opposite and watched the color slowly return to the Chairman's haggard face. The bald-headed leader seemed shriveled and ancient, perhaps aged prematurely by the wire, perhaps by the stress of his Guild position—even with the aid of a computer implant his administrative duties had to be a taxing responsibility, Morvick considered. And was a pleasure wire the reward of success or the price?

Exeter coughed from deep in his lungs and spit phlegm into a pocket rag.

"Now then," he said in rough baritone. "Your report. How is our militia coming along? Did you enlist all those men on Lamarr's list?"

"I did, Father. The group totals sixty-three now, all armed and eager for action. They've been practicing in secret with the laser pistols you supplied and seem reasonably proficient. I think they're ready. Has your spy in the Fraternity found out the final timetable yet?"

"Yes, the cursed wretches have moved the schedule up again. Six cycles is all we have now. The spaceport attack is planned for the very day of the annual sacrifice. The fools expect to strike while the Ra Guild is preoccupied with the sacred festivities. It's an unfortunate inconvenience, but it won't alter our strategy one iota. We'll let our militia handle the dirty work while you and I celebrate safely in the sanctuary with Ra. You have a competent leader in charge, I presume."

"Two, in fact. I've split the group in half to allow for a two-pronged attack on the spaceport—our peace-keeping mission."

"Right." Exeter chuckled. "Peace and harmony for all. We'll have to step up the propaganda now too. Any more ideas along that line?"

"I think we should play up the industrial accidents angle," Morvick replied with easy confidence. "That seems to be where we're having the most success—the heartless corporation negligent in providing safe working conditions for the children of Ceres, the romantic Fraternity struggling to the fore as a type of labor union. We've already got the whole planet talking about mining safety. I've got the latest casualty figures, and I've used the Fraternity deaths to inflate the numbers without actually making any fraudulent statements."

"Great space, Morvick, don't worry about making a fraudulent statement. Lie through your teeth if you think it will help. This is war, for Ra's sake!"

Morvick stared for a moment in puzzlement. All the rules of the game seemed to change every time he turned around. How in space was the Guild to be an improvement over Transolar if they lost their integrity in the process?

"What about our official statement to broadcast Earthside?" the Chairman asked.

Morvick gave his head a quick shake to clear his thoughts. "Not quite finished yet. A lot depends on how the Fraternity attack proceeds—number of casualties and damage reports and such. I've been wondering about the other communication towers, though, Exeter. Our plan focuses only on the main facility and leaves all the other transmitters available to Transolar."

"Yes, but what can they say? Can they deny the Fraternity attack or suggest that it is not in the best interests of Ceres for the Guild to take control of the problem? No, I think they will recognize their inferior position when the smoke clears. Once we gain control of the spaceport with its main broadcast station, we'll have won the battle. We'll have ousted the corporate colonialists forever. Ceres will be ours and ours alone."

"In the name of Ra," Morvick added.

"Of course. Long live the Dragon."

Morvick reached behind his head and kneaded the back of his neck. "Have we examined every possibility?"

"Nothing has been left to chance," said Exeter. "The Fraternity is primed for battle, Transolar sleeps unaware, and our militia is ready to mop up any weary warriors who manage to survive the initial confrontation. What could be easier?"

"I guess you're right." Morvick smiled anew at the simple beauty of their plan. "I picked up the spacer early today."

"Ah, yes, our visiting celebrity. What's he like?"

"A quiet fellow, somewhat reserved. A religious man, strangely enough, a spokesman for some alien gods he calls sprites. He says they claim the entire universe for their very own."

"The entire universe! What manner of gods are these?"

"I don't know. Some type of invisible beings. The fellow himself doesn't seem to have all his facts straight. He maintains that these sprites actually created the galaxies out of vacuum, that their natural reality is of a higher order than the physical plane."

"Nonsense."

"So it appears at first glance. But this spacer seems quite assured of his beliefs. He says it's all detailed in a book, the chapters scattered through the solar system and hand-copied through the ages."

"Bah! I don't believe it. So what does this priest want? He hasn't made any claim on Ceres has he?"

"Fortunately the subject did not arise. It seems, however, that these sprites maintain unofficial ownership over their creation, Ceres included."

"Ceres belongs to Ra alone!" the Chairman bellowed.

"Of course, Father. No need for alarm. The man has made no demands whatsoever. In fact, he seemed terribly naive to our situation here, ignorant of even the most basic realities of colony life. I suppose these mining specialists have only one area of expertise."

"Well, I think we'd better get this all out in the open right away." Exeter rose to his feet and stepped from behind his desk. "He's back at your home in Sector Sixty-Six, is he not?"

Morvick hurried to follow as the Chairman swept across the room and out the door.

Harlin, still dressed in his sky-blue jumpsuit and boots, crept quietly into Marinda's room next door. She was sitting erect at a plain table with her hands folded in front of her, staring straight ahead with wide eyes. Her long black hair was tied in a ponytail behind her. Her skin was white, almost translucent like a fine china doll, her fully dilated pupils as black as space. She did not acknowledge his presence.

"Hi, my name's Harlin Riley. I'm bunking down the hall for a few days, and thought I should introduce myself."

Marinda did not turn her head. She was frozen in a catatonic state by a massive dose of nerveblocks.

Harlin walked up to her and jumped as though to slap her face.

She could not even blink, though she heard every word and could see Harlin vaguely with unfocused peripheral vision.

"Listen," Harlin continued, "I saw your father giving you drugs and it didn't look very pleasant. Frankly, I'm suspicious. Your father says you're sick, but you look pretty healthy to me." Harlin grimaced in thought and shook his head. "There must be some way to communicate with you. Let me see your eyes."

Harlin brought his face right up to the young girl's nose and peered into her black eyes. "If you're being held prisoner here, try to blink an eye for me. Go ahead, I'll wait. Are you being held prisoner?"

Harlin stared, smelling the girl's musky scent, feeling her steady breath on his chin. He thought he saw movement in her left eye. He squinted. Her eye quivered, the muscles struggling to act.

"Okay, I got it," Harlin said, and Marinda relaxed her effort. A lone tear leaked out of her eye and drew a wet line down the side of her face.

Harlin reached up and wiped her cheek with her thumb. "I'm going to help you somehow, Marinda. Whatever's going on here isn't right on any planet. Give me a few days to reconnoiter. I promise I'll come back for you."

With a heavy sigh Harlin began to pace back and forth in front of the girl. "There must be someone you can trust," he said finally. "I just don't know where to begin. Look, I'm going to put a pen in your hand." He pulled a pen from his breast pocket and ripped a piece of paper from his notepad. He placed the pen between her fingers and pointed it onto the paper.

"Try to write a name for me, something to go on, anything. Take your time."

Harlin whirled in alarm as the door opened from outside. His face slipped into a poker mask of innocent tranquility as Morvick and Exeter entered the room and gaped in surprise at him.

"Morvick," he said quickly, striding forward with deliberate calm, "I must compliment your family on the beauty of your child. It is too bad that her mind is not as healthy—she suffers from some form of mental illness, I presume?"

Morvick and Exeter exchanged glances of reassurance. "Why, yes," Morvick said, "a chronic problem. She barely speaks at all."

"Did she say anything to you?" Exeter demanded in his gruff baritone.

"No, not a thing," Harlin replied.

Morvick sighed with relief. "This is Chairman Exeter Englehart of the Ra Guild," he said, holding his left hand out wide.

"Harlin Riley, spider miner." Harlin slid up and shook the Chairman's hand Earth-style as he unobtrusively appraised the man. Stooped with age and wizened by the wire, Exeter had a coarse grey beard and a closely shaved scalp, the scar from his implant operation a large red welt just above the hairline.

"I see you're carrying a computer," Harlin duly noted. "That's pretty rare north of Luna."

Exeter tipped up his forehead in obvious pride. "An implant is an aid I couldn't be without, an absolute necessity for a man in my position."

"The Chairman is responsible for the entire planet," Morvick explained. "He is the intermediary between Transolar and the civilian populace. We really should leave Marinda to her rest, gentlemen," he said as he ushered the two toward the door and into the hall. "My office is in that second door to the left," he pointed. "I'll just check her medication and be right with you."

Morvick turned back into Marinda's room. He could have sworn he had locked the door. He checked his daughter's eyes for signs of life, picked up her wrist and let it drop slowly back to the table. A piece of paper lay under her hand. He examined it and saw the word "Tova" scrawled crudely in a tight pattern. He crumpled the evidence, took a hypodermic from the purse at his waist and stabbed her neck with another dose of nerveblock.

Morvick hurried down the hall to his office and found Harlin and Exeter still chatting about computers.

"So it speaks to you," Harlin was saying, "inside your head?"

"As I understand it, an electrical stimulation causes a pattern of vibrations somewhere in the inner ear," Exeter explained, "which results in a rather crude representation of human speech."

"How can you differentiate your own thoughts from the computer's voice? Doesn't it get rather chaotic in there?"

"No, no, the computer is not sentient, you see. It's just a convenient database, a problem solver. It can't initiate a conversation or come up with an original idea. The computer is after all merely a tool, a mechanical aid. It's hard to describe, but the computer's voice is flat and unemotional, whereas my thoughts are—well—mine."

Harlin grinned. "It must have taken a lot of getting used to."

Exeter smiled and nodded as he remembered some of his early moments with the implant. "It was strange at first, I must admit, but it's second nature to me now." He noticed Morvick standing near the door. "Morvick, come in and sit down. We've just been discussing some technical matters."

Exeter turned back to Harlin as Morvick pulled a chair closer. "But enough about me. I came to hear more about you. Morvick tells me you're a priest."

Harlin straightened in his chair and glanced from Exeter to Morvick and back, wondering what sort of official pogrom might be on their minds. From bad to worse, he considered.

"Well, yes, I suppose I'm a priest of sorts. Every sprite carrier takes that responsibility on himself."

"All priests, eh? Doesn't that cause a lot of confusion? Too many cooks in the galley?"

"Everyone has their appointed task. Everyone works as they are directed by the sprites."

"And just what is your task on Ceres, Mister Riley? You're not here to set up some sort of rival sect, are you?"

"Pardon me?" Harlin stared in surprise at Exeter's quick move to the offensive.

"Well, you arrive here with this—this alien presence. You say in fact that you have been led here by your god. What are we to think?"

"Well, I—" Harlin stumbled as he realized that there might indeed be some hidden reason for his visit to Ceres, some purpose known only to his sprite. Perhaps he was to rescue Marinda and take her to Luna City. "I'm just passing through, as far as I know."

"You have no plans? No native contacts?"

Harlin shrugged. "No, I'm really just waiting for a ride home."

"Fine." Exeter displayed his finest committee-meeting smile. "Then let me officially welcome you to Ceres on behalf of the Ra Guild." He extended his right hand again, and Harlin stood up to shake it. "We will do our best to make your stay a pleasant experience and will try to secure your passage offplanet at the earliest moment possible."

"Thank you. I'll try to stay out of the way." Harlin turned to leave.

"And don't you worry about our pretty young thing down the hall," Exeter added, causing Harlin to stop in his tracks and face the Chairman again. Exeter tapped the side of his forehead twice and gave Harlin a knowing smile. "She's under the best medical care available."

"No harm done," Harlin replied. "I hope she responds to treatment."

"We're not holding much hope, but you never can tell. Miracles are our business after all, are they not?"

"Indeed," Harlin murmured, and shuffled out of the room, thinking again about miracles, about the tumbling dice of destiny.

Rick St. Ames stared glumly at the ticker-tape reports on his flatscreen monitor as a large block of Transolar Corporation went by at eighty-eight dollars a share. He ran his fingers through his thick green hair and shook his head. Rick had sold out a month ago in the low seventies following the lead of Andy McKay, but it looked as if Andy had goofed this time. The price of Transolar had been rising steadily as demand continued to outstrip supply. A three-for-one stock split was rumored to be in the works, and Rick knew the rumor alone could push the stock up over the hundred-dollar barrier. He debated whether to start buying again. What was it Andy had been worried about? Something on Ceres? Rick struggled to remember the details. Maybe he should give Andy a call, he considered. He hadn't talked to him in weeks.

The light on his phone flashed yellow. "Rick St. Ames," he answered with bland formality.

"Hi, Rick."

"Diane." He'd know that satin voice anywhere. "Well, speak of the devil."

"What?" She sounded alarmed.

"Just an expression. You okay?"

"No. You haven't heard?"

"Problems at Night Sky?"

"Worse. Have you seen Andy?"

"Not recently. Not since our night flight. He said something about going Earthside for a holiday. On a canoe trip, I think it was. Did he not come back?"

"He hasn't been in the office for over a month. His secretary has been hospitalized because of overwork. I'm at Andy's desk now trying to patch things up. I need your help."

"You mean he disappeared somewhere in the Canadian wilderness? Have the authorities been alerted? Call the Prime Minister."

"No, no, Rick. He's not hurt—not physically." Diane sighed. "He called me from some plebeian outpost at the edge of nowhere about two weeks ago. He proposed over the telephone and I turned him down."

"No."

"Rick, I just couldn't do it. He sounded crazed and manic, and we had a bad connection. It just didn't seem like the Andy I know."

"He should never have put you on the spot like that. Not over the telephone," Rick agreed. "Maybe he's sick. Maybe his doctor has prescribed something for a medical problem. That would explain everything. Maybe he's picked up some rare disease from Earth."

"He's sick all right. I think he's had a complete nervous breakdown."

"Let's not jump to conclusions."

"You haven't heard the worst part yet."

"There's more?"

"I have in my hand a faxed invoice from a Korean manufacturer for a fully reconditioned atomic freighter—a Class Seven Starship. Guess who's signature is at the bottom of the contract?"

"An atomic freighter!"

"Still think I'm overreacting?"

"What does he want an atomic freighter for?"

"I was hoping you might tell me."

"That's a pretty expensive proposition," Rick considered, his skin suddenly prickly with heat.

Diane laughed, her mirth void of music, a harsh, tense laugh in which the fear was only barely concealed. "That's right. And guess who's holding the bag?"

"What are you going to do?" Rick thought out loud.

"I'm going to watch you dance, little man. You're his best friend and chief financial wizard."

Rick was sweating now, his mind racing. He wiped the sheen off his brow up into his thick green hair.

"Don't sign anything. Don't negotiate with anyone. Our story is that Andy is on holiday, living it up on some Brazilian beach with all the other mega-millionaires. Where's the freighter?"

"Space only knows. It left the dock weeks ago. I feel so helpless, so useless. It's a bad way for the company to end."

"Hey, hey, let's not cut our blasters yet. We don't even know if there's a problem here. Andy could've flipped this baby at a big profit for all we know. It could have changed hands two or three times by now. You remember how he used to work in the old days? He used to scare us silly. Just sit tight, baby. We'll ride this one out in style."

"You think so?"

"Damn straight. Fax me some numbers and I'll shift some money around for a smokescreen. That'll hold off the creditors until Andy shows up." What was he saying, Rick wondered. He didn't believe a word of it.

"Thanks, Rick. You're a dear. I knew you'd think of something. I just hope Andy's not in some kind of trouble. What if he's been kidnapped or blackmailed or something?"

"I'm sure he'll be all right," Rick offered half-heartedly.

"On the telephone he asked me to pray for him. Well, I've never prayed for anything in my life, but I'm about ready to start now."

"Sounds worse all the time, Diane. Maybe he has burned a few circuits. Don't take it too hard though. A girl like you can get a job anywhere. You can come and work for me if you like. Your voice on the phone lines would double my commission income."

"It's not the job, Rick. It's Andy. I'm afraid I may have hurt him. Or maybe he thinks he has to prove something to me. I just wish I could have the old Andy back. I just pray that he's safe."

"Pray if you like, but I hardly think it will make much difference. Let me see what I can do at my end."

Rick cradled his phone with a worried frown. What a mess. Andy had always been a bit eccentric, even before the megabucks had started to accumulate, but a disappearing act like this was way out of character. Foul play was possible, Rick considered, but there was no sign of a ransom note or any of the demands usually associated with a celebrity kidnapping. And what would anybody want with an atomic freighter when Space Navy already had a monopoly on all long-distance transport? The whole idea was crazy. The mad millionaire was writing a brand new chapter on the midlife crisis.

Diane's faxes came in and Rick whistled as he began crunching the numbers. He pulled up Andy's files on his computer and started work on a complicated analytical spreadsheet. He popped two antacid tablets in his mouth and began chewing, then washed them down with a cup of black coffee. His phone flashed.

"Rick St. Ames."

"Mr. St. Ames, this is Sergeant Carruthers over at Space Navy Control. I have a patch-through relay from an unregistered vessel for you personally. The pilot's name is Andy McKay."

Rick choked on his coffee. "Put him on," he coughed. The red-haired wonder had finally surfaced.

"Substantial charges will accrue to your account, sir."

"No problem."

"Fine. If you'll hold the line, I'll signal Mister McKay to begin transmission. There's a three-minute time delay each way due to the limitations of the speed of light. Please hold on."

Confused at first, Rick quickly grabbed a pencil as understanding dawned. Three minutes each way! Great space! The speed of light was one hundred and eighty-six thousand miles a second. In three minutes that was over thirty-three million miles. Rick gaped in disbelief as the numbers registered in his brain—that was a third of the way to the sun. Or outward almost to the orbit of Mars. By all the gods of space!

"Hello, Richard. This is Andy. I guess you've probably figured out where I am by now. I'm at zero-g and weightless, but the computer tells me I'm making good speed." Andy chuckled—not his usual hearty and carefree laugh, but the forced cackle of a man who knew he'd put himself in a ridiculous situation, tense and full of self-doubt. "I'm giving you official approval to sell everything in the ISS portfolio as market conditions will allow. Fax the documentation to my secretary, Valencia, as the money starts coming in. Keep Night Sky until the last, or ask Diane if she wants to buy me out. Please confirm reception. Over."

Rick bit his lip. What does one say to a crazy man? Turn around and come home quietly?

"Sure, Andy, whatever you say. Valencia's out of the picture, though. She couldn't take the pressure. Diane's in the driver's seat at the moment. The Koreans are pressuring her for some big bucks, buddy. We're both looking for an explanation. Over."

Rick sat back in his chair as the enormity of his situation struck him. Here he was conversing on the telephone with a lunatic over thirty-three million miles away. He imagined the pulsed laser beam as it sent his voice out into the heavens, bouncing off Space Navy freighters like a billiard ball looking for a corner pocket in the dark. He switched the phone to a desk speaker and hung up the receiver. He started in again on the spreadsheet before him, but couldn't keep his mind on target. The whole scenario looked like an unforgivable waste of money, a wanton blasphemy in Rick's book. The very thought made him feel sick to his stomach. He didn't mind paying for little frills and pleasures along the way, but numbers with zeros behind them were holy—part of the business cycle and not to be tampered with unproductively. He checked the ticker-tape on Transolar and saw a block go by at eighty-eight and a quarter. The stock was still rising, Rick noted sullenly.

A crack of static announced the incoming transmission. "It's a long story, Rick. I know it looks a little foolish, but I just can't explain the whole thing right now. Sometimes you can't judge everything in dollars and cents. I'm sorry to hear about Valencia, but I'm happy Diane's taking some interest. Maybe she still cares about me after all. When this is all over, will you be the best man at our wedding? Over."

Rick bent his head into his hands and massaged his forehead above squinting eyes. Marriage! Andy had really blown his fuses this time. Stay calm, he told himself, stay cool.

"Andy, I'm not sure she's going to go for this wedding stuff after hearing about your little joyride. You used to have such a good head for business; I just can't believe what I'm hearing. You can't go running off like some fool kid on a new bicycle and leave us to pay the bills. I've been working on your spreadsheet and I haven't got enough numbers to fill the holes. I can't see anything but trouble with a debt-load like this. When are you going to wake up? Over."

Rick got up to pour another cup of black coffee, muttering and complaining to himself under his breath. Six minutes was too long to wait for an answer from a crazy man. It left him too much time to think, too much time to worry. A man spends his whole life scratching and saving, sacrificing everything to get ahead, to build a little nest egg for a comfortable retirement. Then he gets up one morning, makes one false move and it's gone, just like that. If it could happen to Andy, it could happen to anyone; that's what upset Rick the most. He had spent years looking up to Andy, brainstorming with him at expensive nightclubs, partying till dawn. They had built careers by directing the course of business events instead of just reacting to old news like everybody else.

"I just did wake up, Rick. I'd been asleep for years."

"Oh, spare me the cheap philosophy!" Rick interjected, then realized that Andy's transmission was still on the air. He wrestled with his temper. Damn it, money was important. Mystical jargon was cheap and worth even less.

"—and tell Diane to stall the Koreans. I'll figure something out. I really appreciate you, Rick. You've always been there for me and I owe you bigtime. Stick with me for a few more weeks. I can always start again if I have to. We'd better close this connection before the charges put us both in the red. Over and out."

"Fine, Andy. Drop in and see me the next time you're passing through this part of the solar system. Over and ended."

Rick slammed the top of his speaker phone and stared at it in grim disbelief. The lunatic Andy was worried about the price of a phone call while he frittered away millions of dollars. It just didn't scan. And this was the man on whose advice Rick had sold all his Transolar stock. Rick pondered the fact glumly. Andy was obviously burned out—space salad for brains.

Rick punched up the ticker-tape on Transolar. The stock had closed at eighty-eight and three-eights, up three-eights on the session. A thousand shares would cost just under a mega. Rick could swing it if he borrowed half the money. A three-for-one split could make for a big move in the price of the stock. He'd read all the reports. He knew the company inside out. Transolar was a good investment.

Rick put a buy order into the computer for the next morning—ten thousand shares at market—and started clearing up the paperwork on his desk. Always best to go with one's own instincts, he told himself, a satisfied smile slowly spreading on his face. After all, numbers never lie, and a man's mind is his only real oracle from the heavens.

PART FOUR

Harlin woke to find a man shaking him by the shoulders, a frail man with a wispy black beard, a red-robed skeleton with hollow cheeks and dark, sunken eyes.

"Wake up, Earthman. The girl needs you now."

"What girl?" Harlin muttered as he rubbed sleep from his eyes.

"Marinda told me you promised to help her. Does the promise of an Earthman truly mean nothing these days?"

"Marinda? Do you know where they've taken her?" Harlin stood up. "Is she all right?"

"She is about to be executed, my friend. Only you can save her. You must get her offplanet within twenty-four hours."

"By all the gods of space! What are you saying?"

The mystery man held up a hand to still any questions. "I'll explain as we go. Pack all your belongings and follow me. Vast forces are converging around us, and we haven't much time."

Out in the hallway the man pulled a knife from his red robe and offered it to Harlin, a short, sharp blade with an ornately engraved handle. Harlin held both palms up in front of him.

"The girl will be tied with ropes," the man persisted, pushing the knife into Harlin's hand. "You'll need the blade to cut her free. You shall not have to kill anyone if we are lucky. I have a better method of dealing with the guards."

He reached into his robe again and produced what looked like a bracelet—a gossamer thread with a single pendant, a silver thumbtack. He slipped the strap around his hand so that the sharp tooth pointed upward in the center of his palm.

"This needle contains a powerful nerveblock, not fatal, but extremely debilitating for up to fifteen hours. We will each have one of these, for there are two men standing guard. All you need do is grab the guard's arm with this device in your hand and hold him steady while the drug takes effect. Four or five seconds should do it, but grab the guard's gun hand just in case."

"I can't," Harlin complained as they skated briskly along. "If I get involved in any violence here I might never get offplanet. All I have is a conditional visa."

"The stakes are high, friend. Do you know what they do with the sacrificial virgin once they carve her to pieces?"

Harlin stared at the treadway in front of him, afraid to meet the thin man's haunted eyes. A hand gripped his shoulder and pulled him to a halt. He looked up.

"They cook her, friend Harlin. They eat her flesh and drink her blood."

Harlin gagged as his stomach boiled inside him. He stared into the stranger's dead black eyes and saw the truth inscribed with pain. The bracelet dangled in front of his face like the pendulum of an ancient timepiece. Wordlessly Harlin reached up and took it.

A promise was a promise, he told himself as they continued down the long tunnel, wondering if he would ever get offplanet after this escapade. His muscles tingled with tension as they approached the two Ra Guild guards. The tableau appeared dreamlike, removed from reality and somehow absurd. He steeled his body for action, clenching himself like a fist.

The sentries recognized the mystery man and voiced polite greetings. The red-robed figure greeted them back nonchalantly. Harlin, starkly out of place in his azure jumpsuit, elicited a puzzled look from one of the guards. The man opened his mouth to speak, but never got the chance; the mystery man had him by the arm. Harlin lunged and grabbed the other guard, sending them both somersaulting in the low gravity. By the time they hit the wall opposite, the sentry was limp below the dazed spider miner.

Harlin stood up and palmed the door sensor. He stepped through the open iris to find Marinda sitting in a chair in the center of the empty room, her arms tied behind her back.

"Earthman!" she exclaimed. "I'd almost given up hope."

"You can speak," Harlin noted with a grin.

"Yes, the drugs have worn off."

Harlin looked around behind him. The red-robed stranger was gone.

"What are you waiting for?" Marinda demanded.

"I thought another man was with me," Harlin told her in confusion.

"A friend?" Marinda asked, and peered at the doorway with concern.

Harlin shrugged. "He led me here and took out the guards."

"Cut these ropes quickly. I don't like the sound of this. You do have a knife, don't you?"

Harlin bent behind her and cut her bonds. She stood up and ran to the door, reached down and snatched the two laser pistols from the unconscious guards. She handed one back to Harlin.

"What do I need this for?" He handled it at arms length like a poisonous snake.

Marinda looked at him in amazement. "Do you know how to shoot?" she asked.

"No. Do you?"

"No, but I'm willing to learn fast if I have to. Let's go."

She moved stealthily down the hall, and Harlin followed for no particular reason that he could think of. He wondered whether he was a criminal now according to native law.

"Where are we going?" he asked the girl.

"Be quiet!" she hissed.

A beam of focused light flashed just inches over her head and sizzled on the wall above her. She ducked and rolled away. Harlin turned to look at the source of the blast and saw a third guard standing over his two prone comrades, his outstretched arms leveling a laser pistol at Harlin's head. It took Harlin a full second to grasp the situation. That man's going to shoot me, his mind screamed, but his body seemed unwilling or unable to respond.

Marinda dragged him down as a sparkling thread of light passed over his shoulder. She fired a blast at the guard, who ducked in the open doorway. Harlin crabwalked to the first corner and dove for cover. Marinda rolled onto his lap. They gasped for breath.

"Thanks," Harlin said. "You saved my life."

"We're even," Marinda responded. "That guard seemed to be aiming at our heads. The others won't make the same mistake. Try to stay alert."

The suggestion was unnecessary. Harlin could feel the blood singing through his veins like an electric current, his mind in a state of hyperactivity, half-formed ideas fighting each other for his conscious attention.

Marinda jumped to her feet. "Come on, Earthman. We've got to get out of this sector before they seal it off."

"My name's Harlin. We haven't been properly introduced."

"Fine, Harlin," Marinda said as she pulled him up. "Let's not waste time."

A siren began to wail in the distance as they hurried down the rocky corridor.

"What's that?" Harlin shouted, his nerves ajangle.

"Our friend has reported us. It won't take the Guild long to get a guard at every station. We may have to shoot our way out."

Harlin looked down at the laser pistol in his hand. His blanched reflection stared back at him from the polished chromium. He wanted to throw the gun away but dared not. It seemed a link to life somehow, a magic charm.

A closed airlock blocked the tunnel ahead, a red light flashing above the door.

"Flame," Marinda cursed. "They're overriding the airlock computers." She approached and tried the sensor pad. The door refused to move. She turned back to Harlin, her face already relaxing into sad apathy. "I think we're going to die now, Harlin."

He looked back over his shoulder—no guards in sight yet. "We could give ourselves up," he offered.

"Yes, they might spare your life, but I'm afraid you know too much for them to ever let you go. And of course I am overdue on the altar already." She smiled with an unexpected shyness, her cheeks lightly colored. "Thank you for your help, Harlin. It's a shame you didn't bring a god from Earth to fight our dragon."

Harlin's sprite twisted within him, a persistent tickle that forced him to speak. "I did bring a god, Marinda."

Marinda's eyes opened wide in surprise, then she smiled in disbelief. "You carry one with you everywhere you go, right?"

Harlin's sprite fairly cartwheeled in his abdomen, making him feel giddy with excitement. He chuckled. "Well, you never know when you're going to need one," he said.

Marinda frowned and turned away. She pressed both palms against the closed airlock door, pushed back and forth several times, slowly rocking. She turned back. "You're serious?"

"By all that's holy, I swear."

Marinda squinted at him, her eyes running the length of his body, peering behind him, around him.

"The sprite is invisible to you, Marinda. It lives inside me. You can have one too, if you like. The sprites offer eternal life to all who carry them."

"Eternal life? Right now I'd be happy to see my twentieth birthday."

Harlin glanced behind him for any sign of guards or soldiers. "I'm not sure the sprites can help us out of this predicament, but if we're going to die anyway we might as well have somewhere to go."

Marinda shook her head. "I'm not worthy enough to have a god inside me."

"You are," Harlin insisted. "No one is too small or too great. A simple invitation is all it takes. They don't take up any space. They rarely interfere. I've carried one for years."

"And this sprite will make me live forever? It sounds too good to be true."

"I don't understand the mechanics behind it, but somehow the spiritual union produces a new creature that survives bodily death. The sprites consider the symbiosis to be their natural state. They're incomplete without us."

Marinda's mouth drew a firm line of determination. "All right, let's do it. We may not have much time. How do I get their attention?"

Harlin's sprite tumbled and trembled within him. If ever he had felt the hand of destiny, it was now.

"There is a sprite here waiting for you."

Marinda froze and looked slowly up. "I'm afraid," she whispered. "What do I say?"

Harlin shrugged. "Something from the heart. They don't use language. They know who you are, all about you. Just be honest with them."

Marinda bit her lip. She closed her eyes above sweat-pebbled cheeks.

"I invite you in," she whispered. "I know I don't deserve to live forever, but I offer you everything I have." She opened her eyes. "Was that okay?" she asked.

Harlin grinned, his sprite vibrating with exultation. "Just great," he told her. "Congratulations. May I give you a hug?"

Marinda looked at him doubtfully. "Is it customary?"

"Not exactly. Just a welcome to the family."

"I don't feel any different."

"You just don't know what to look for yet. You'll notice him eventually."

"Are you sure it's not a her?"

"Technically, I don't believe they're gender specific. As a matter of fact, the sprites may not be strict individuals the way we imagine. They're all connected somehow."

"One hug." Marinda held a finger up with a smile.

They folded together like family. Marinda was the daughter Harlin never had. He felt complete, at peace with the universe, ready to die once again.

"Hey!" Marinda pulled back. "I just remembered a dropshaft that we used to play in as kids. There could be an access hatch near here. We may be able to get up a level or two." She scanned the hallway, trying to gauge directions against the vision in her mind.

"This way," she said as she began dragging Harlin down a small side corridor.

"Won't the Ra Guild have closed it down too?" he asked as he ran beside her.

"The hatch opens outward from the shaft, so it seals automatically against vacuum on any level. I'm sure it'll be unlocked. I can just see it."

She dodged down another corridor to the left. Harlin went wide in the low gravity, his feet flailing empty air, and hit the wall at full speed. Marinda skidded to a stop and turned.

"You all right?"

Harlin stood up gripping his right shoulder, wincing with pain.

"You've got to stay on the treadway," she reminded him.

"I know, I know," he muttered as he moved to follow her again.

Another quick turn and they found their objective. Marinda pried open a spring-loaded trap door on the wall to expose a porthole about fourteen inches in diameter.

"I'm not going in there," Harlin told her flatly.

"Why not?"

"It's too small."

"Nonsense. You can squeeze through."

Harlin peered inside. "It's dark," he complained.

"Close your eyes and you'll never know," Marinda suggested.

"What if we get stuck in there?"

"The walls are smooth. Are you finished?"

Harlin cocked his head sidelong at her, arms akimbo.

"I'll go first," she said. "Hold the hatch for me." She poked her head in the hole, reaching upward. Her torso disappeared, her hips caught briefly, her legs kicked into darkness.

Harlin sighed.

Wake up, fool. Wake up and know the wrath of Ra!

The stimulation stopped abruptly as Exeter was jolted back to reality by the voice inside his head. Fear gripped him like clammy hands tightening on his spine.

"What is it?" he whispered. There was no one else in the room.

Treachery and deceit. My virgin has been stolen. I hold you personally responsible. The inner voice screamed with arrogance, vibrating the bones of his skull—not the voice of his computer implant, nor his own thoughts, but something altogether different, something alien and horrible.

"Ra?"

Of course, fool. I utilize the device in your feeble brain to communicate with you. Stop your quaking and obey my commands. Treason surrounds us like the fires from heaven. Hurry to the spaceport before all is lost. The Dragon will not be outwitted by human scum.

Just then Morvick rushed into the Chairman's office to find Exeter holding his head with both hands, staggering blindly in a circle. He grabbed him by the shoulders and shook him hard.

"Exeter! Marinda has escaped with the spacer priest!"

The Chairman threw off his hands and pushed him away. "I know, fool, I know," he shouted, his face pasty white. He scurried over to his desk, pulled a laser pistol from the top drawer and tossed it to Morvick. "Your eyes are better than mine," he said. "Hurry now to the spaceport. She'll be trying to get offplanet." His bald head bobbed through the door as he lumbered from the room with his crooked back stooped like an ape.

Morvick's knuckles clenched white on the pistol as he followed close behind.

"Where is our attack force now?" Exeter yelled back over his shoulder. "Have they engaged the survivors yet?"

"They're on their way to the spaceport. The Fraternity has the whole planet in an uproar. They're advancing on every major installation. There are hundreds of them, thousands. Our propaganda has worked to perfection. The chaos escalates just as we planned."

"Let's hope the girl doesn't upset our strategy."

"What could she do? She's only a child."

"I don't know, Morvick, but Ra is worried about something. We'll have to kill the Earthman now of course."

"Of course," agreed Morvick.

Dead bodies lay strewn like broken dolls on the upper levels, the air hazy with smoke and the smell of charred flesh. Most of the dead wore standard beige coveralls with red Transolar insignias, but a few black Fraternity uniforms sprinkled the group. The corpses seemed undamaged at first glance, but on each was the telltale black thread of laser disruption, the purple blisters of internal hemorrhage, the face contorted in grisly agony. The stench of death hung in the air like a funeral shroud—blood and fire and vapor of smoke. The two Ra Fathers gagged as they ran, stumbling over corpses and sweating from the infernal heat.

Morvick stopped in surprise as he noticed a familiar face in the carnage—a young boy that had gone to school with his daughter, his black Fraternity uniform still smoking with heat, his dead mouth twisted in a crooked grin. Morvick knew his parents, had fed the boy at his own table. He stared aghast at the sight, wondering how such a young life could be wasted like this. He tasted bile in his throat, the horror of war suddenly vivid before him. No more a game of political strategy and tactical maneuver—now suddenly a dead baby, a mother's son caught in something he would never understand.

"Morvick, what is it?" Exeter demanded from down the tunnel.

"A boy from my parish," Morvick replied vacantly.

"Morvick!" Exeter yelled. "I hear fighting up ahead in the main hangar."

Obediently Morvick stumbled forward, his gullet raw with acid. He coughed in a futile effort to clear the lump in his throat. His eyes stung with smoke.

"You go first," Exeter commanded, pointing through an open airlock, his voice thick and acrid like the polluted air.

Morvick stepped forward cautiously and looked out into the large repair hangar where the battle raged. The Guild militiamen were off to the left, a small cluster of red-robed figures holding a position among some metal-working machines, laser blasts leaping from their arms like long swords of fire. Two portable pulse-cannons stood in their corner like huge guards dogs, periodically crackling with energy as they discharged violent bursts of electrically charged particles. The Fraternity defended the upper levels of the hangar, armed only with laser pistols, their tiny black shapes swarming along the balconies and guardrails and flying like shrapnel when the lightning bolts exploded among them. Transolar Security was nowhere to be seen.

"Where did the Fraternity get so many men?" Exeter asked as he crept up behind Morvick to view the scene. "It will take forever to clean them out of the Control room up there. Where's the rest of the Guild militia?"

"They should be advancing from the other side." Morvick pointed to the far right. "Up from that conveyer belt in the corner." No red robes were visible yet in the area.

"Let's get over there and see what's holding them up." The Chairman ducked back into the open airlock.

Morvick surveyed the battle again before hurrying to follow, convinced that his pincer attack would quickly end the exchange.

"Who's in command of the other regiment?" Exeter asked as he shuffled awkwardly down the rocky corridor.

"Your secretary, Lamarr," came the reply from behind.

"A competent man, but perhaps a little young for such responsibility," the Chairman commented grimly.

"He's twenty-eight years old, Exeter, and he seemed to know most of the men. You yourself suggested he be involved."

"Yes, yes, I'm sure he'll be along presently. Does he have any pulse-cannons with him?"

"Yes, two more."

"Fine, that should quicken things up. We've got to get control of that transmitter as soon as possible."

"I suppose the Fraternity is on the air now," Morvick noted, feeling a knot of tension in his abdomen.

"It looks that way. Good evidence of destabilization for any Earthside listeners, though I'm surprised that Transolar could be overcome so easily by a bunch of boys. That must be why Ra is worried."

"How do you know Ra is worried?" Morvick asked uneasily.

Exeter grimaced, his temples still throbbing with pain. "The Dragon has his ways. Don't ever underestimate him."

Morvick nodded in agreement. It would be foolish to underestimate a god. After all, gods were gods, not weak and fallible like men. Who could stand against Ra the Dragon? Who would dare to question his will?

The Chairman and his Prime Minister arrived at the other end of the hangar just in time to see a squadron of red-robed soldiers and two heavy pulse cannons rolling in on the conveyor. Anchored by four thick, hydraulic legs, the cannons were silvery with a faint blue patina, the core discharge tube a crystalline jewel.

Lamarr directed his troops with the precision of a trained general as they readied the cannons for battle. A short, wiry man with a sparse black beard, he looked like a skeleton, with dark, sunken eyes and parchment-pale face.

Chairman Englehart strode forward to address the troops, but stopped short in surprise when, as if on cue, the soldiers suddenly began fighting among themselves. Several men fell forward unconscious, drugged by nerveblock, and the survivors ripped off their red robes to reveal black coveralls beneath. The powerful pulse-cannons sprang to life with a crack of thunder. Twin lightning bolts licked out like a forked tongue of fire, a solar flare of annihilation streaking across the cavern. Caught unexpectedly by the surprise attack, the Guild militia at the far end of the hangar had no chance to return the fire before their guns were disabled.

"Lamarr!" Exeter cried in fury. "What treason is this?"

Lamarr tossed his red robe to the floor and turned to face the Chairman. He raised his laser pistol, but did not fire. Seeing that Morvick was dangling his own weapon uselessly at his knee in bewilderment, Lamarr lowered his pistol and approached the two Ra Fathers.

"I'll tell you, Exeter, now that our victory is assured." His voice brimmed with anger, with a hate he had kept contained for years. "Her name was Danielle. Do you remember?"

A look of guilt flashed across the Chairman's face—a stab of private pain.

"Remember with me, old man. Your own daughter, Danielle. We were to be married, but you stole her away and killed her on your ghoulish altar."

"Not I," Exeter whispered. "The Dragon's will."

"You sold your own daughter for political power. You sliced her up to gorge your own putrid belly. I've waited a decade to repay you—a life for a life."

Exeter's eyes bulged with panic. He looked around wildly. "Shoot the traitor, Morvick. This is the treachery Ra warned about."

Morvick stared from Exeter to Lamarr and turned in surprise as Marinda and Harlin raced through a nearby airlock and stopped abruptly. Marinda instinctively raised her weapon, but she also did not fire, confused by the scene before her. Harlin began to back warily away.

"Another daughter for the sacrifice, Morvick?" Lamarr asked softly.

"Morvick! Don't be a fool!" Exeter shouted. "Shoot the traitor. He's sold out to the Fraternity."

The skeleton in black coveralls laughed mockingly. "I created the Fraternity, Exeter. My men call me Tova—perhaps you've heard the name. You helped a good deal yourself, though you didn't realize it at the time. Did you really think I was your secret spy in the dark? Did you think I would betray my countrymen to a vulture like you?"

"No," the Chairman choked. In desperation he lunged at the laser pistol in Morvick's hand. "It's not too late, Morvick."

The two men struggled briefly before the Prime Minister pushed the Chairman away and tossed the laser pistol to the ground.

"It was too late long ago, Exeter," he said with sad finality.

"May Ra show you no mercy," the Chairman cursed. His lips moved just a tiny bit as he signaled the computer implant in his brain. His eyes rolled up into his head as he slipped under the wire.

"For Danielle's sake, I silence you," Tova stated as he raised his weapon and fired.

A few ragged cheers sprang up from the balconies above as the Chairman's lifeless body hit the ground. A few men shouted instructions as they began to extinguish the small fires that had been kindled by the cannons.

Tova surveyed the scene with grim satisfaction. He strode up to Morvick, the confident air of victory like a crown upon his head. "The day is coming and now begins when the red robes of the Guild will be no more," he declared.

Morvick shivered with a quick swell of fear. Who could stand against the Dragon? Who would dare to question his will? Surely not this skinny man before him.

"It is no easy task to turn around when you are rushing headlong in the wrong direction," Tova warned.

Morvick nodded, considering the consequences of his actions. He removed his purple sash and silver belt and threw them to the floor in front of him. A gold chain followed and clattered on the tarmac. He grabbed his ceremonial costume by the collar and ripped it down the front. He pulled it off his shoulders and tied it at his waist on top of his rough-knit white shift. Tova smiled in salute and turned back to his men.

Morvick faced his daughter and held his arms out wide, and immediately she ran to accept his invitation. They embraced wordlessly, their eyes wet with emotion, cherishing the moment like lovers reunited. Harlin smiled happily at the turn of events, thinking he might get off this planet in one piece after all. More importantly, a sprite had been planted like a seed and would be nourished in a fertile environment. Harlin quietly dropped his laser pistol and knocked it away with the toe of his boot; he was an innocent bystander once again.

But Harlin's sprite began to squirm energetically inside him, refusing to let him relax and enjoy the scene. Something was terribly wrong. Voices began shouting at the far end of the cavern, and all eyes turned toward the source of the confusion to see the Dragon himself advancing like a monstrous demon from the very bowels of hell, his eyes glowing like molten metal, his jaws the color of fresh blood, his six huge arms gesticulating wildly, razor-sharp talons slicing the air. The ground shook as he bounded closer on sturdy iron legs. His tail whipped from side to side, caving in steel walls and bending huge structural supports with each wicked blow. He roared the angry battle cry of an ancient warrior, the sound of a raging wind-blown fire.

Tova was the first to react, already moving while others stood paralyzed with fear. "Ready the cannons," he yelled back over his shoulder as he darted toward the beast. With a laser pistol in each hand, he fired squarely onto the Dragon's chest, but though the scaly skin smoked red with fire, the beast never faltered. Like a locomotive the Dragon continued forward, his gruesome roar raised one notch louder by the pain.

Tova redirected his aim for the eyes and sent a beam of focused light straight up into each red orb, but still the Dragon did not flinch. In a moment Ra was upon him. A giant arm swiped downward with talons outstretched and murdered the Fraternity leader with a single quick blow.

A pulse-cannon barked as a lightning bolt caught the Dragon full in the throat, momentarily stunning the beast in an explosion of electric fire. Ra howled in anger and advanced on the machines. Another lightning bolt hit him, this time lower on the chest, and again his skin glowed crimson and he screamed like a demon in pain. He staggered back and almost fell, but his heavy tail stabilized him. He howled and leapt forward. He pounced on the pulse-cannons and crushed them like tin cans as the Fraternity brothers fled into the tunnels in defeat.

The silence was eery. Invincible his power, Ra the Dragon had come to reclaim Ceres for his very own. He bellowed in victory as the laser fire ceased, his voice like the sound of a spaceship engine blasting off.

"Worship me, foolish mortals, and I will spare your wretched lives!"

No one made a move to answer. Morvick, Marinda and Harlin stood off to one side with a few Fraternity survivors. Others watched from balconies and upper windows, hundreds of tiny black figures standing motionless in witness to the horror below.

The Dragon let his gaze wander around the hangar as he surveyed the cowering onlookers, his metal skin still smoking hellishly. He snarled when his eyes met Harlin's.

"Well, Prophet," he growled with a voice dripping venom, "what have I to do with you?"

As everyone turned to stare in astonished silence, Harlin seemed to be suddenly transformed by the attention, empowered by some hidden resource. Weaponless, he stepped out boldly to face the Dragon. He planted his feet firmly and folded his arms in front of his chest, a man assured of his destiny and embracing it gladly.

"Your time has come as it is written," he said simply, and the few who were close enough to hear his small voice gasped at the sheer audacity of the spacer priest.

The Dragon blinked in disbelief. His chest rose with gathering fury. "Prepare to die, little man," he blared.

The prophet closed his eyes and raised his hands above his head. His lips moved as though conjuring unseen powers, in prayer perhaps or incantation. The air around him seemed charged with magic, sparkling and turning like the glinting facets of an invisible jewel.

The Dragon shrieked his foul battle cry and charged at Harlin with talons splayed, wailing and gnashing his daggerlike teeth, but as he approached his skin began to glow as if a hundred pulse-cannons were trained upon him. He screamed in ghoulish anguish and stopped short of Harlin. He circled the prophet, writhing and screeching in anger. Harlin held his ground and smiled with gathering power, transported into an unknowable spiritual reverie.

The Dragon wheeled around looking for an opening, his skin smoking cherry red, his demonic wail rising in both pitch and volume as tiny tongues of fire began to dance on his body. He closed his eyes and ducked down, his jaws wide open. He lunged straight into the spinning diamond of light and snapped his teeth onto Harlin's body with a crunch of broken bone. A blinding flash of light engulfed them both and sent a cloud of white smoke to the ceiling. Bits of molten metal rained throughout the hangar, sticking to flesh and clothing and burning holes wherever they landed. No other trace was found on Ceres of Ra the Dragon or the spacer priest.

At every major Transolar installation around the planet, Fraternity lieutenants waited patiently for the retreat code that never came. The remnants of the Ra Guild forged a hasty alliance with the Fraternity, and the new republic sent out a radio broadcast claiming sovereignty and political independence. In the name of human rights and freedom they announced a new age and offered to negotiate new contracts on all mineral sales.

The reaction was swift and harsh, the official Transolar statement terse and uncompromising: under no circumstances would the Corporation negotiate with criminal elements or revolutionary groups, nor be swayed by subversive propaganda or threats to company hostages. All colony support was immediately withdrawn and a blockade put in place to all spacecraft.

The Corporation had a cold, titanium heart. With numerous other colonies scattered among the asteroids and Martian moons, Transolar had no choice but to set a firm example. Too much was at stake to risk a hint of weakness. Billions of dollars had already been lost as the price of Transolar stock had plummeted on the capital markets. Any further loss of confidence would ruin the company forever. A few weeks without water rations would bring the new republic to its knees groveling for mercy. Transolar still held the upper hand and they knew it.

At the first sign of trouble, Transolar staff had started vacating the planet. Shuttles packed with personnel had lifted off steadily while the Fraternity advanced. Virtually every navigable spacecraft had been commandeered for the exodus, from geologic scanners to medical lifeboats. Emergency radio channels were clogged with chattering voices awaiting rescue by the single Space Navy freighter enroute. Many of the craft were manned by unauthorized pilots and were veering off on strange trajectories away from Ceres. The Space Navy Commander complained to Head Office that he'd need a butterfly net to catch them all. An emergency team was working round the clock to pinpoint targets and plan logistics for a huge rescue operation.

The Fraternity brothers eyed each other with faces of hard granite, the vacuum in their hearts like a bottomless chasm. Their leader was gone now, though it seemed doubtful that even the master dreamer would have had a strategy for this situation. Tova had been only a man like themselves, after all. Now they had only legendary figures to cling to, martyrs who had sacrificed their lives without qualm: the short, wiry skeleton who had thwarted the designs of the Ra Guild, and the spacer priest from Earth who had fought the Dragon unarmed and vanquished him with the power of the stars. The reins of power fell by default to Drako, a young mechanical engineer who had proved himself an able leader in battle. He kept Marinda and Morvick at his side as advisors, and together with a handful of Fraternity lieutenants they set up a Command Center in the Transolar offices at the spaceport.

Reports began to trickle in as the Fraternity brothers took stock of their resources. Huge stockpiles of metal were on hand, of course, and Marinda's reports from the hydroponic gardens indicated an ample food supply. The critical factor, however, was water. Several storage tanks had been sabotaged by Transolar, and others were near empty. An order went out to begin reclaiming water from the gardens immediately. Even so, Drako calculated, within five days water rations would be cut off entirely. In five more days the weakest colonists, the elderly and young children, would begin to die.

"There's not a single ship on the docks, sir," reported a young lieutenant, Bardock, "not anywhere on the planet. Transolar took every last one into orbit. We can't get an envoy out. We can't get a mineral shipment to market."

"Very good, Bardock," Drako replied without emotion.

"Can we barter with a neighboring asteroid?" Marinda asked.

"Not with the Transolar embargo in place," Drako pointed out. "Deimos is close this time of year, but two of the three outposts there are Transolar affiliates. Space Navy will be watching their skies for anything unusual."

"We could beg for help from Earth," Bardock offered. "I'm sure the big civil rights groups would give us a receptive hearing."

"They would. Some have contacted us already. But they're deep in the gravity well," Drako explained. "It would take several weeks to get anything to us."

The Command Group lapsed silent as they considered their fate. Space was too big. Ceres was an isolated colony on the edge of an ice-cold vacuum. They were all born into slavery and destined to die.

"We should give in to Transolar," Morvick spoke up. "The Dragon is gone now. I'm sure the Corporation will deal fairly with us. The longer we wait, the harder it will be for everyone."

After a moment's silence, Bardock cleared his throat noisily. "I'm willing to face execution if it means my children can live, sir."

Drako looked up to meet Bardock's steely black eyes. He searched from face to face among the Fraternity lieutenants, and shook his head sadly. He turned to Marinda. "The spacer priest and his invisible god," he said quietly, "what would they have done?"

Marinda felt her sprite stir within her for the first time, like a young child stretching in the crib. She shivered with awe and delight at the experience.

"I say let's wait," she replied.

The Control operators heard the news first when a request for landing clearance broke the radio blackout. A space freighter appeared like magic on the short-range radar. The pilot called himself the Cosmic Cowboy and laughed like a mad fool. Everything had fallen into place like a jigsaw puzzle for Andy McKay, and he couldn't help but laugh. On his long trip out he'd spent a lot of time wondering about a fool and his money, about madness and folly. Perhaps sanity was only a relative construct anyway. It sure felt good to let loose a belly laugh again.

"Cosmic Cowboy, this is Ceres Control. We've got you on our board and you're clear for landing. We can hardly believe it down here. Over."

"Believe it, Ceres Control. I've been following your situation for days, but felt it wise to maintain broadcast silence until I ran the blockade. The cops were all out chasing butterflies. Listen, I've never landed one of these tubs. I need computer up-link for a Class Seven Starship, unregistered. I'm running Techtronix software in a Korean mainframe made by Global Systems. Can we lock some hardware, or what? Over."

Drako stood panting beside the radio operator, having run from his office to the Control room when he heard the good news. He watched two Fraternity brothers as they poured through manuals and punched at their keyboards to interface their equipment with the renegade starship.

"Up-link on the way," the Control operator spoke into his microphone, and Andy's board began to light up like a Christmas tree. "Our Governor would like to have a word with you, Cosmic Cowboy," the operator said, and handed the microphone to Drako.

"Sir," Drako spoke, "we welcome you to Ceres at a turning point in our history. We are in a critical situation here and need your aid. Over."

Andy laughed happily, relishing the moment. "Thank you, Governor. Tell your people my cargo holds are full of water, the most valuable commodity in the universe. I repeat, pure Canadian H-Two-Over."

Andy howled with joy as the garbled mayhem of celebration sounded in his headphones. His sprite danced a dervish twist inside him. "Whoever is thirsty, let him come," he said to himself.

The landing lights blinked on. The cyclopean spaceport opened its armored eyelid to reveal the docking pad inside. On the shore of space the lighthouse winked.

Harlin Riley woke to find himself lying face down on a smooth, hard surface like a sea of glass, the gentle pressure flattening his nose and cheek. He soaked in the feeling of gravity like a man pulling a breath of fresh air deep into his lungs. He listened to it with his arms and legs as it cajoled him from below. He tasted it with his lips. He was happy that heaven had a sure foundation.

Death lay safely behind him now, the last battle fought, the last foe conquered. In the back of his mind lingered the faint memory of a dream—a dream of bathing in a pool of crimson and coming out clean, his life left behind as a dirty rag, an abhorrence. Like a newborn babe, innocent and unsullied, the essence of Harlin Riley had been salvaged.

Even as he lay there with his eyes closed, he could see the light. He could feel the emanation near his head, softly stroking his face like a warm, velvet blanket. For a moment he was content to bask in the experience, as the first thrill of his resurrection surged like electricity through his regenerated body.

Finally Harlin opened his eyes and blinked as the glorious light flooded into his soul. A man stood nearby, his two bare feet incandescent like burning bronze, radiating gentle warmth and glittering like polished gold.

In awesome terror Harlin cast his eyes up, pushing his head and shoulders from the ground. The man was dressed in a linen robe, clean and white, with a golden sash tied around his waist. His hair was white also, like a virgin snowfall, his eyes aflame with fire. His face glowed with the light of a hundred suns, transcendent in the beauty of holiness. Rainbows danced around his head like halos, reminders of promises kept and sure words never broken.

Overcome by the scintillant presence, Harlin fell back to the ground and covered his face with his hands as if to hide from the unspeakable glory of his god like a pauper cringing from a rich man's finery.

But the heavenly being smiled and reached down with nail-scarred hands to help Harlin to his feet. In a voice like the sound of many rushing waters—mighty waterfalls, cascading mountain streams, and bubbling musical brooks—the god-man spoke.

"Well done, faithful servant. Stand up now; it's almost time to begin."

"And there was war in heaven: Michael and his angels fought against the dragon; and the dragon fought and his angels, and prevailed not; neither was their place found any more in heaven. And the great dragon was cast out, that old serpent, called the devil, and satan, which deceiveth the whole world: he was cast out into the earth, and his angels were cast out with him.

Therefore rejoice, ye heavens, and ye that dwell in them. Woe to the inhabiters of the earth and the sea! for the devil is come down unto you, having great wrath, because he knoweth that his time is short."

Revelation 12: 7-9,12.

About the Author

Born in Brampton, Ontario and educated at the University of Toronto, Steve Stanton began writing seriously soon after his graduation in 1978. His short stories and articles have been published in Canada, United States, England and Australia.

A preliminary draft of *In the Den of the Dragon* was originally penned in 1983 and was revised and updated periodically for a dozen years. Excerpts from this novel first appeared in *The Standing Stone #1*, copyright 1990, Toronto, Ontario, and *Dreams & Visions #7*, copyright 1991, Washago, Ontario.

Steve Stanton has lived and worked in the Orillia area for twenty years. His ancestors Thomas Stanton, Sr. and Mary nee Winter immigrated to Orillia in 1860 from Chesterfield, Derbyshire, England.

Coming Soon From Skysong Press

SUPERLIGHT

A New Novel By Steve Stanton

In a technologically advanced future, a new blood-transmitted virus has appeared on Earth, a "reverse-AIDS" virus that causes the immune system to regenerate the body, vastly prolonging life and creating a small and growing group of infected Eternals. Are they a biological menace or the next step in human evolution?

Zakariah Davis, a virus carrier and gifted cyberspace cowboy, must track down the Source of the virus and will stop at nothing to secure the truth. The future of Earth depends on it; the space-time continuum is cracking under pressure. Death will never be the same.

Release Date 1997
Reserve Your Copy Now
At Special Advance Pricing

Yes, I would like to order **SUPERLIGHT** at the Special Advance Prepublication Price.
I have enclosed $6.95 for a First Edition copy.
SKYSONG PRESS, 35 Peter St. S., Orillia, ON L3V 5A8